GONE FOR YOU

A Wild Side Novel

RILEY HART

Cover Design by X-Potion Designs
Cover Image by vishstudio
Edited by Flat Earth Editing. Proofread by Flat Earth Editing and Judy's Proofreading.
Artwork by Sarah Jo Chreene

Dedication

For Andy. The idea for this book was born on our night out in West Hollywood. I might have gone overboard creating my own history from a story you told. I hope you enjoy seeing a romantic get his very own happily ever after.

PROLOGUE

Ten Years Earlier

"JESUS CHRIST, YOU'RE staring at Matt like you're gonna walk over there and start humping his leg any second." Miles crossed his arms and looked at Oliver as though he was ridiculous.

"Or raise your leg and pee on him. You know, to mark your territory. Get your scent all over him so people know he belongs to you," his friend Chance added because obviously, they thought Oliver needed both of their opinions. Chance winked a purple, eyeliner-traced eye at him.

"Only he doesn't. Belong to him, I mean. Matt's great but he belongs to whoever he thinks can get him what he wants, Oliver. It's time you realize that. I—"

"That's a little unfair, don't you think?" Chance cut Miles off. Oliver's eyes darted between his two friends as Chance continued, "You never know, maybe he harbors a ridiculous, secret crush on Oliver the same way Oliver does him." Chance smiled at Oliver as though he'd done him some kind of favor. He hadn't.

"Gee, thanks. I've always wanted to be called ridiculous by one of my best friends. You're a pal. And I don't have a secret crush on Matty—fuck you both very much." He was lying his ass off, and they all knew it. He had an absurd crush on his friend he needed to get over.

Or do something about.

Chance and Miles let out boisterous laughter he could clearly hear over the loud music of the party. They were eighteen—not old enough to get into the clubs they wanted to go to but young enough to crave being drunk every chance they had. This was basically their weekly routine.

"You're such a fucking liar," Chance told him and yeah, he was the biggest fucking liar there was. He wanted Matt and had for years. He glanced at both men, Chance with his short hair dyed the same purple as his makeup. He had a baby face, round, with eyes full of mischief. Miles was the opposite, always brooding with his hard, square jawline and buzzed hair, his skin shades darker than Chance's.

"I'm thinking about telling him tonight." Oliver took a drink of his vodka with cranberry and orange juice, and an added dash of grenadine—a drink the group had named *Morningstar* after a night of too many of them—while he waited for his friends to lose their shit. Logically, he knew telling Matt he wanted him was dumb. Matty had never shown the slightest interest in him that way. Matt would hook up with any guy that walked but he'd never so much as given Oliver a second glance. It was a great ego booster.

"Go for it," Chance said at the same time as Miles's, "No…no, no, no. That's a very bad idea, Oliver. Actually, it's the worst idea you've ever had. It could be the worst idea anyone in the world has ever had."

"What the fuck?" Oliver shoved him. "It can't be that bad!" People had crushes on their friends all the time. It was one of the most popular tropes there was, and considering Oliver wanted to be a writer, he paid attention to that shit.

"Yes, it can," Miles told him. Oliver looked at Chance, who nodded his head in agreement.

"You just told me to go for it!"

Chance exhausted him sometimes.

He shrugged in reply. "I wanted to be supportive."

Jesus, he hated his friends. Oliver looked over at Matt again. He had his back against a wall, a cup in his hand while he talked to another man who stood beside him. Matt's brown hair hung over his forehead, but he kept pushing it back. Even though he couldn't see them from here, Oliver knew Matt's eyes were this wild, almost seafoam green. He had long, dark lashes, really kissable lips, and dimples that brought Oliver to his knees.

Matt was fucking beautiful. Everyone who looked at Matt thought he was. Matt knew it too. It was a fact.

They'd known each other since they were about twelve, but they hadn't been good friends at the time. Matt's mom had worked for Oliver's parents. She'd cleaned their house and sometimes cooked meals for them. Every once in a while, she'd brought Matt with her and he'd always looked fucking miserable—not that Oliver could blame him. Matt hadn't gone to school with Oliver, Chance, and Miles. He'd lived on the other side of Los Angeles. It couldn't have been fun for him to be there while his mom cleaned someone's house.

He'd tried to get Matt to hang out with him but at first, Matt wanted none of it. Eventually, he'd come around. It had taken him longer to warm up to Chance and Miles, whom Oliver had known practically since the day he was born.

They were different...so fucking different, but their differences had never mattered to Oliver. Matt was his boy. Nothing would come between them. And hell, if Oliver had silently been in love with him for years, how did he know Matt didn't feel the same? Maybe he'd kept it to himself too.

"You do know he plans to fuck that guy he's talking to, don't you?" Miles asked. He always put things out there like that. Brutal honesty was Miles's thing, even if people sometimes thought it made him a dickhead.

"Well, maybe I'll tell him and we'll be fucking each other instead." Or at least he'd get this heavy-ass weight off his chest. If it sucked him down any more he'd drown.

"He knows. You have to realize he already knows," Miles added because apparently, he felt like it was a fun night to stab Oliver in the heart. Repeatedly.

"What? How could he know? He would have said something if he did."

"Because everyone knows?" Chance asked. When Oliver looked at him, he held his hands in the air as though he was waving a white flag. "I'm just sayin'."

Yeah, he really fucking hated his friends right now. "Thanks for the vote of confidence, guys. I appreciate it." Oliver walked away, ready to find another drink.

The thing was, he'd been thinking about telling Matt for a while now. They'd just graduated high school a few days before. Their crew had their whole lives ahead of them. Matt and Oliver planned to get an apartment together for college. Oliver, Chance, and Miles were going to USC, and Matt was going to a local community college. Why not start off with a bang?

Oliver made his way to the kitchen and got another drink. He finished it, surprised that Miles and Chance hadn't come to hunt him down. As soon as he stepped out of the busy room, he ran right into Matt's chest. His friend's arms reached out. His hands curled around Oliver's biceps.

"Hey, man. I was looking for you," Matt said.

"Where's the guy you were talking to?"

Matt shrugged. "Eh, he wanted to hook up, but I wasn't in the mood. Wanna go outside with me?"

Oliver's heart went crazy, while he felt ridiculous for it at the same time. Maybe his friends hadn't been so wrong calling him that. But the truth was, Matt just skipped out on a hookup to find him, and now he wanted to go talk.

Holy shit. What if he was right? What if Matt felt the same way he did, and he planned to tell Oliver tonight? They'd ride off into the sunset together—or you know, take a dirty, piss-scented bus through the city, same thing—before they went home, had wild, passionate sex, and lived happily ever after. Fuck Miles and Chance. They had no clue what they were talking about.

"Earth to Oliver. You in there, boo?" Matt snapped his fingers in front of Oliver's face.

He did that sometimes—spaced out—probably because he felt so much freer in his imagination than he did in reality. "Yeah, sure, yeah. Let's go talk." God, he sounded like an idiot.

Oliver followed Matt outside. It was still in the eighties out, even though it had to be close to midnight. He loved summer in LA—sunshine and warmth. It was perfect.

"Let's sit," Matt told him before sitting on the top step. Oliver went down beside him. "Are you having fun?"

Was it him or did he hear a slight shake in Matt's voice? Plus, what the hell kind of question was that? Matt had never pulled him aside to ask him if he was having fun at something. "Um…yeah. Are you okay? You're being weird." He was acting nervous. Matt didn't get nervous.

He nudged Oliver's leg with his own. "I should have known you'd realize something was up. I…I gotta tell you something and it's kind of hard to say."

Oliver's heart dropped to his feet. *Holy fucking shit.* Matt wanted him too. He knew it. That had to be it. What else would he be nervous about saying? "Come on, dude. You know you can tell me anything. I…I think I know what you're going to say."

Matt's green eyes went wide. "You do?"

Oliver nodded.

"You're okay with it? I don't want anything to fuck up our friendship."

Fuck you, Miles. Fuck you, Chance. He wants me. "Nothing would ever screw up our friendship. I love you, Matt."

"Whew!" Matt let out a deep breath. "I've been losing my mind thinking about telling you. I mean, I know we swore we were going to get an apartment together but I just…I can't wait to follow my dreams, ya know?"

Oliver's gut clenched. That wasn't what Matt was supposed to have said there. "Wait. What?"

"I already got the bus ticket and everything. New York Fucking City. I can't believe it. My parents lost their minds when I told them, but I knew you'd understand." Matt wrapped an arm around Oliver, pulled him close, and kissed his forehead. "I know it's going to be hard. The guy who's letting me stay with him—I met him online—said I only have a month, which is pretty fucking scary, but I've always wanted New York City. I'm thinking I can take a year off, write a bunch of music and then maybe get into the New York School for Music. My parents, they don't get that. You're my best friend, Oliver. I knew you'd have my back."

Best friend. New York City. The guy who's letting me stay with him. Matt was leaving. He was really fucking leaving. And he hadn't told Oliver until now. He had plans, a place to stay, bought a bus ticket—all without telling Oliver.

They were supposed to get an apartment together, party, enjoy their fucking lives, and Matt was leaving? "Why didn't you say anything earlier? I could have planned to go with you. We both could have planned to go to school out there instead. Maybe after a semester or something, I can transfer."

He pulled away to look at Matt. The porch light shone on Matt's face.…On the soft curve of his jaw, the roundness of his lips, and the dimple beneath his mouth. Jesus, he was fucking beautiful.

His brows pulled together and he darted his eyes away. Oliver realized like a punch to the gut that Matt didn't want him to go. He hadn't told him because he wanted to leave Oliver behind.

"I just…I wanna do it on my own, ya know? I want to take this adventure on my own to see if I can do it—without you fixing things for me."

Oliver nodded, but he didn't know. He really fucking didn't.

Eight Years Earlier

OLIVER'S PROFESSOR GAVE him the evil eye as he snuck out of class early.

He shrugged but kept going. He couldn't help it. Traffic was a bitch, and he needed to get his ass on the road so he wasn't late to pick up Matty at LAX.

Oliver looked forward to visits from Matt. Oliver, Chance, and Miles still got together often. It wasn't always easy, but they did it. With Matty being in New York, they were only able to meet up with him once a year. That was a whole hell of a lot more important to him than studying the Revolutionary War.

He'd missed Matt while he was away. It didn't matter that they talked all the time. It wasn't the same, and as much as he loved spending time with Chance and Miles, that wasn't the same either.

Like he knew it would be, LA traffic was hell on Earth. It took longer than expected to get to the airport, but even with his stop to grab Matt his favorite coffee, he still made it before Matt's flight landed. He'd planned ahead to give himself plenty of time.

Oliver had the whole week scheduled out. Matt would stay with him; they'd go to all their favorite places. He'd made sure to clear his week to spend much needed time reconnecting with his closest friend. They'd get together with Miles and Chance too, of course, but he hoped to get a lot of one-on-one time in as well. Maybe then he would be able to talk to Matt about school. It had been two years, and he wasn't doing anything with his music. Oliver got it— shit like that was hard, but he knew how much Matt wanted to compose. Matt deserved to have his dream.

He finally made it into the airport, cold coffee in hand. He should have waited until after picking Matt up.

Oliver leaned against the wall. A good half hour passed before he saw the dark head of hair he would know anywhere. "Matty! Hey!" Oliver made his way through the crowd and toward his friend. Matt looked up and smiled the smile that nearly knocked him on his ass every time. Yeah, he was so totally fucked where Matt was concerned.

"Hey! Oliver!" Matt made his way to Oliver and pulled him into a hug. He smelled like cologne that Oliver didn't recognize. Still, he held tight, happy to have his friend back, even if it was only for a week. "It's good to see you," Matt told him.

Oliver closed his eyes, held tighter and said, "It's good to see you, too, Matty."

When they pulled away, Oliver looked over to see a blond guy watching them. Um…what the fuck? Oliver was about to ask the guy if he had a problem when Matt glanced over and smiled at him. "Oliver, this is my friend Jeff. Jeff, this is Oliver, the guy I told you about."

Oliver's gut twisted. This was a new development. He'd never heard of Jeff but apparently, Jeff had heard of him. He sure as shit didn't expect Jeff to be here—what? For the week with them?

"Hey, man. Nice to meet you." Jeff held out his hand and an immature part of him wanted to ignore the man. But that wasn't his style, so he gritted his teeth and held out his hand when he would much rather have punched the guy in his smiling face.

"Nice to meet you too."

"Thanks for letting me crash your visit at the last minute. I appreciate you being willing to let me stay with you."

It took everything inside Oliver not to whip around toward Matt and ask him what the fuck this was about. "Yeah. Sure. No problem," he said between tight lips.

Jeff went to get his bag, and Matt wrapped an arm around him. "Thanks, Ollie. I knew you wouldn't mind. Sorry I forgot to ask you. It's okay, right? I mean, if not, Jeff and I can probably find a hotel or something…"

A hotel? What the fuck was that about? Matt was supposed to stay with him. "What? No, it's fine. No problem." Oliver's muscles were tight as he spoke. His stomach rolled uncomfortably.

"Thanks. I appreciate it. I've been telling Jeff all about LA. He's never been. I figured we could show him around, take him hiking and shit like that. It'll be a blast. The more the merrier and all."

Oliver tried not to groan. "Yeah, the more the merrier." So much for one-on-one time with his best friend.

Six Years Earlier

OLIVER WAS HALF-ASLEEP when his phone rang. He rolled over in bed, eyes burning as he squinted so he could see. Jesus. It was three in the morning. Who the hell would be calling him this early?

He nearly knocked the phone off his nightstand before he managed to pick it up. When he did, he saw Matt's name on the screen. "This better be good," he said into the phone.

"It's fucking fabulous is what it is. I just landed a modeling gig, Ollie. A good one. Can you believe it?"

Oliver sat up, a mixture of happiness and confusion fucking with his already tired mind. Matt had never once mentioned modeling. It hadn't even been on his radar, yet he sounded happier than Oliver had heard him in years. "Wow…that's…wow. That's incredible.…It's incredible, right?"

"Yeah! This is fucking big. I feel like I'm going to lose my mind here. I want to shout it from the rooftops; I did it, Oliver. I fucking did something for myself and you're the first person I told. As soon as I found out all I could think was, *I can't wait to tell Oliver.*"

Fuck. Oliver's pulse started running a race. If he were a cartoon character, there would be floating hearts by his head right now. He was fucking crazy over this guy and it needed to stop....But when Matt said shit like that to him? How in the hell could he put on the brakes?

"Thank you. I'm so proud of you. This is only the beginning. I know it." And he did. Matt could do anything he set his mind to. If Matt decided he wanted to model instead of compose, Oliver was happy for him. "I can't wait to celebrate with you."

The line was quiet for a moment and Oliver knew exactly what it meant.

"I don't think I can come...not right now. Maybe later in the year, though. There's too much going on for me to get away."

Oliver dropped his head back against the headboard. What Matt said made sense. It did. And he understood. This was Matt's livelihood. He had to do what was best for his career but damn, he'd looked forward to seeing him. "I could try to come to you. It might not be next week because I didn't plan for it but—"

"Yeah, yeah. That'd be cool. Maybe. Let's talk later in the week, okay? I mean, if I'm busy with work I don't know how much time I'll have anyway. Maybe we could plan something in the next few months."

This was only the beginning of canceled trips and Oliver knew it. Again, he understood. They had lives and responsibilities. It wasn't like everyone got to fly across the United States to see their best friend every year, but damned if he didn't think it would be different for him and Matt.

Just as he opened his mouth to respond, to tell Matt they'd been friends too long and they should find a way to see each other, a voice in the background stopped him. "Matt! What are you doing? I'm horny. I want my dick in your mouth before I fuck you. Get your ass back in here!"

Oliver felt like he was going to be sick. Not that he thought Matt wasn't hooking up. Why shouldn't he? He was a single, sexy-as-hell man. Plus, it wasn't like Oliver was a virgin either. He got his. He doubted as often as Matt but he got it when he wanted it. But really…had he snuck out on a hookup to call him? Oliver wasn't sure if he should be annoyed or feel special.

"Listen, I better go. I'll call you soon, okay? And thanks for understanding, Oliver. I love you."

He had no doubt Matt did love him. Matt had always loved him, only not in the same way Oliver felt for him.

He closed his eyes, wishing like hell Matty didn't own such a big piece of landscape in his heart. "I love you, too."

Four Years Earlier

MATT STOOD ON the balcony of his agent, Parker's, apartment—the party Parker had thrown for Matt buzzing around him. They'd been working together for about two years now, ever since Matt realized the guy who had supposedly scored him his initial modeling gig was nothing but a fraud who couldn't deliver when it came to work but liked the idea of having a pretty boy on his arm. Matt had spent a few months being that man.

Christ, he should have fucking known.

He couldn't believe he'd been dumb enough to fall for that shit. It hadn't been the first time he'd been used or taken advantage of, but he made sure it was the last. He'd been so fucking embarrassed he'd let himself get taken advantage of, but he'd been so desperate at the time. It had come down to making some money or packing his ass back to California where everyone would know he'd failed.

Where he'd have to look Oliver in the eye and tell him he couldn't handle it. He was determined to make something of himself on his own and now he was doing that.

Matt took a bite of the dessert in his hand. It was chocolate and caramel, sweet as hell, but damn, it tasted good.

"Oh God, that looks fucking incredible." Santiago, one of Parker's other clients, approached him.

"It is." Matt smiled at him. He'd always had a sweet tooth, especially when it came to chocolate or marshmallows. "You're not having any?" he asked and Santiago shook his head.

"Fuck, no. I feel like I'm going to gain five pounds by looking at it." Both men laughed as Matt felt the warmth of another body step up beside him. It was Parker. He wore a suit that likely cost more than anything Matt had ever owned back home. He looked innocent as hell with his red hair and freckled nose.

"You have a little chocolate right here." Parker reached over and swiped at Matt's bottom lip and then held his hand there and nodded toward his finger. Matt grinned at him before he sucked the tip of Parker's finger into his mouth and licked it clean.

Santiago chuckled, turned and walked away.

"Are you having fun?" Parker asked.

"Of course," Matt told him. "Thank you for this."

Parker waved off his thanks. "You look great but then that's no surprise. You're always gorgeous. Jesus, there are so many people interested in a piece of you."

There was a slow churn in Matt's gut he tried to ignore. This was a good thing. People wanted him. He'd actually fucking done something with his life.

He was able to help his parents now.

He was in a beautiful apartment in Manhattan at a party being thrown for his modeling success and the campaign he'd just landed. His heart pulsed with an emptiness left by the fact that Oliver wasn't here to see it. He wished like hell his friends could see what he'd done but then wondered if he really had the right to feel that way at all.

CHAPTER ONE

OLIVER SAT WITH Miles in their booth at Wild Side as they watched Chance dance on one of the tables in front of them. Chance was an incredible dancer. Everyone in the bar—men and women alike—seemed to agree, as they shoved money into his underwear. Chance rubbed his hands down his body, looked at Oliver and ran his tongue across his top lip.

Oliver rolled his eyes at his friend. "He's popular," he said to Miles even though they both knew he was.

"He's ridiculous."

"You like that word."

Miles looked at him and smiled. He still wore his suit, likely because he'd just left work. Still, he was here. This had been their spot since they turned twenty-one. Chance had been dancing here on Saturday and Sunday nights since he was twenty-three. Five years was the longest Chance had stuck with anything besides their friendship. Their Friday night routine always happened, even when Chance picked up a Friday night at work like he did tonight.

"It's a good word," Miles said, pulling him out of his thoughts. He rubbed a hand over his short, dark hair. His eyes were whiskey colored, his brown skin a shade or two darker.

"How's work going?"

Miles shrugged. "All right. I'm on a big case, so things might get a little hectic for me."

Miles was a highly sought after LA defense attorney. He always won, which fit Miles to a tee. There was never a doubt that Miles would go on to be successful. He was a slight workaholic and would be a full-fledged workaholic if it wasn't for Chance and Oliver. "Did he do it?" Oliver asked with a grin, knowing Miles wouldn't answer. He only rolled his eyes at Oliver who laughed.

"How's it going with the guy?"

Oliver groaned, knowing that subject would come up eventually. It always did. "I don't understand the fascination with my social life."

Miles took a drink of his rum and Coke before swirling the rest around in his glass. "That's because most of the time I'm too busy to have a social life of my own, and Chance's is too hard to keep up with. That means you're stuck with the focus on you."

Oliver couldn't help but laugh. It was true—Chance definitely loved the social aspect of his job. He enjoyed men a lot more often than Oliver or Miles did. Probably more than Oliver and Miles combined. Miles meant to let loose a little more than he did but yeah, the workaholic thing. And Oliver? Oliver was the fucking romantic. He sort of hated that about himself sometimes. It would be easier if he just wanted to fuck anyone he saw…anyone with a cock, at least, but that wasn't him.

Most of the time the group lived vicariously through Chance or when they caught up every few months or so from a phone call with Matt. He hadn't been out to visit in a couple of years. His modeling career was going great, which still surprised Oliver—not that Matt was doing well but his career choice. He couldn't remember the last time Matt mentioned music, but he guessed people changed. Their dreams changed too. Most people weren't stuck in the past the way Oliver was.

"So, the guy?" Miles prompted, speaking over the music. Oliver looked up just as Chance turned to face them, smiling as a guy stuffed money into the back of his underwear. His dyed-blond hair hung in his face in a way Oliver would think was sexy as hell if it wasn't Chance. Miles and Chance had never been anything but the best of friends to him. One couldn't afford to be attracted to more than one of his friends and that had been reserved for Matt.

"Hello? Earth to Oliver." Miles snapped his fingers in front of Oliver's face.

Oh yeah. The guy. He shrugged. "The guy is a guy. I don't know. It's only been a few weeks."

"A few weeks is longer than most of your relationships." Miles finished his drink and leaned back against the half-circle booth, putting his arm around Oliver.

"I'm not sure I'd call it a relationship." They'd hung out a couple of times was all. "His laugh drives me batshit crazy, and he does it all the time. He obsessively chuckles at everything. He has this fucking...gurgly-rumble thing at the end of his laugh like he has phlegm in his throat. Jesus, is it possible to have mucus in your throat all the time?"

Oliver looked over at Miles, who frowned at him then cocked his head. As he did, Oliver's words ran through his head again and the duo burst out laughing.

"Do you hear yourself?" Miles asked, obviously amused by Oliver.

"Yes! Shut up. It's gross." Was it too much to ask to find a man without phlegm? They were in LA, for crying out loud. There were beautiful, smart men around him all the time and he ended up with a guy who gargled snot when he laughed.

"What about when he gives head?" Miles asked, still laughing. "Now that would bother me. Mucus and cock don't go hand in hand."

Oliver leaned back in his seat, clutching his stomach, he laughed so hard. "Jesus, now I'm not even going to get a blowjob out of the deal because I'll be afraid he's going to spit his phlegm on my dick."

15

"What's so funny?" Chance plopped onto the seat beside Miles. It must be his rotation off, which meant he'd get to sit a few songs out. His skin glistened with sweat from having danced so much. The eyeliner around his eyes ran slightly, and the light glinted off the glitter on his face.

"Wait? You haven't gotten head from him yet?" Miles asked Oliver before his eyes traveled in Chance's direction. "He's making up reasons to dislike the new guy, and apparently they haven't even gotten to the sucking stage yet."

"Really?" Chance asked just as Oliver said, "I'm not making anything up, and I'm going out with the guy tomorrow night. If he doesn't sound like he has pneumonia when he laughs, I'll let him suck my dick. Are you guys happy now?"

"I'm hoping you'll be the one who's happy after getting your dick sucked. Been a while for you." Chance grabbed Oliver's cup and finished the drink in it.

"Thanks. I wasn't drinking that or anything," Oliver told him, and Chance kissed the air toward him. His friends drove him crazy, but he loved them.

He knew the men were partially giving him shit, but at the same time, they didn't really get it either. Sometimes Oliver didn't get it. It wasn't as if he never got horny. It wasn't that he didn't want sex. He just didn't like sticking his dick in random men—or having random men's dicks in him. Was that so weird? To not want random hookups or to use apps to make human connections? Sometimes he felt like he was in a different universe from most of the people he knew.

"You look mad. I didn't mean to piss you off. I'm just being real." Miles raised a brow at him, and Oliver nodded because he got it. He'd known Miles his whole life. The man wasn't going to change. He would always tell it like it was.

"He's not so bad besides the laugh. He's having me over to his place tomorrow night. Cooking me dinner." Eddie was a nice enough guy. Oliver liked him…all right. He just wasn't sure he could like him for longer than a few more weeks. He couldn't help it if he was particular about who he spent his time with.

"You're so fucking picky," Chance told him. "It's sex. Or blow-jobs. Or hell, just a date. Have a little fun."

"There's nothing wrong with being picky, and so is he," Oliver nodded at Miles who spoke next.

"But we're not talking about me. And I agree, there's nothing wrong with being picky to a certain degree, Chance. Oliver doesn't stick his dick in anyone; you're the opposite. Both of you should just become obsessed with your work like me."

Chance ignored Miles.

Just then, Dare, the owner of the bar, approached their table. They'd gotten to know him fairly well in the years they'd been coming to Wild Side. He'd recently gotten into a relationship with his friend, Austin, who made appearances every once in a while.

"Chance, do you mind going back out? Tony fucked up his ankle," Dare told him.

Chance stood. "No problem."

"Thanks, buddy. I owe you," Dare replied before saying hi to Miles and Oliver, turning, and walking away.

"I'll see you guys in a bit," Chance said. "But I'm glad you're going out, Ollie. It's been a while since the last time you dated. Maybe you've been waiting your whole life for a guy with a fucked-up laugh and he'll sweep you off your feet or whatever the hell it is you're waiting for."

He kissed Oliver's forehead; then did the same to Miles before he was gone, making his way through the crowd, and Oliver was left wondering if he was truly creating a reason not to like the guy. It wasn't a crime to be particular about the kind of man he wanted to date, and as nice as Eddie was, he just couldn't see himself being with the guy very long, which honestly made his gut cramp. Jesus, maybe he was too picky.…Maybe he shouldn't be thinking *long-term* and should be thinking *next orgasm* instead.

"He likely has allergies. A little nasal spray might fix the guy right up," Miles said, and Oliver started to laugh again, but he didn't really feel it, and he couldn't say exactly why.

CHAPTER TWO

NOTHING FELT RIGHT anymore. Matt couldn't put his finger on what it was, but an emptiness had been slowly eating away at him for too long. He smiled when he was supposed to and laughed when he should. He and Parker went out with their friends and still fucked when they felt like it, but Parker had been playing on the side a little more than usual lately. Matt couldn't blame him. He wondered why he didn't want to play more himself, but even that felt like it took too much energy.

He couldn't get into work. Parker was on his back constantly about all the jobs he'd turned down recently. When his contract with Max Cologne expired, he'd turned down everything Parker had sent his way.

Max had expected a lot out of him. He'd done it because there wasn't a choice. He thought by slowing down on the jobs he took, he would feel like he could breathe again, like the heavy weight that always sat on his chest would lessen, but it hadn't yet. He still felt like he was suffocating, the same way he did every time there was a camera on him.

Matt looked around the apartment he shared with Parker—at the custom crown molding and the windows overlooking the city. It was the kind of place he'd dreamed of living in when he was a kid. He lived the kind of life he'd always wanted, so why didn't it feel as good as he thought it would? Why did he feel so...empty? Why didn't he feel the way he thought he would? Like he was *more*?

A noise came from the hallway and he looked over just as Parker stepped out of his office.

He was a beautiful man—tall, self-assured. He looked like he belonged on the beaches in LA that Matt had left behind but also had a sophistication to him that Matt wasn't sure he'd ever possessed. A confidence that oozed off him. Parker would never feel sorry for himself the way Matt did.

Still, they'd always gotten along well. They'd wanted the same things in life—freedom, fun, success—but where Parker felt satisfied, Matt didn't.

"Why are you sitting here with the lights low?" Parker asked as he moved Matt's way.

He reached for the lamp but stopped when Matt said, "The lights from the city make it bright enough. I like to look out and see how alive it is all the time."

"I know you do," Parker replied, then sighed, walked over and sat next to Matt on the couch. "What's going on with you?"

"I don't know," he answered truthfully. Nothing had changed recently. It was just that the feeling of emptiness had managed to spread through him. Had gotten stronger to the point where Matt couldn't ignore it. "I just feel like I'm in a funk. I'll get out of it."

"Jayden called. He asked if we wanted to hook up next weekend. Could be fun. We haven't played together in a while."

He should jump at this idea. He really should. It was just sex. He and Parker had always seen it that way. They had rules in place and it worked for them, but the idea didn't set his gut on fire the way it used to. "We can if you—"

"You're not happy." Parker cut him off. Matt closed his eyes and let out a deep breath before he turned sideways on the couch to face his boyfriend.

"I should be. I don't know why I'm not." He paused and then added, "You aren't either." It was different with Parker than it was with Matt. He was happy in his life, in his career, but Matt wasn't naïve. He knew he wasn't giving Parker what he wanted the way he used to. Matt didn't feel like he was getting it either, which shouldn't be the case because again, nothing had changed.

"I don't know what's wrong with me." He turned back toward the window and dropped his head against the back of the couch. "It's not just with you."

"I know." Parker put a hand on his knee. "I'm your agent. I can see you aren't happy at work too, but right now this is about us. I care about you, Matt. You know that, but I think we need to be real honest with each other right now. Things haven't been good for a while. We need to face that fact."

Matt waited for the fight to rise inside of him. If there was one thing he had always been able to say about himself, it was that he was a fighter—but nothing came. No ideas, no arguments, no pleading or will to find a way to make it work, just sadness and a twinge of regret. "I'm sorry."

"Don't be." Parker nudged him. "Plus, I'm the one who's breaking up with you. We had a good run, but I think the important thing right now is you figure out what's going on with you."

I don't know what's wrong with me.

But he wished he did. He should be more grateful for his life than he was. He'd come from nothing, had nothing, been the kid who didn't really fit in, even with his best friends and now he was *wanted* for God's sake. He had an expensive apartment in New York City with his boyfriend. His fucking face was on billboards.

Why do I feel so empty?

"Have you talked to Oliver?" Parker asked.

"Huh?" Matt frowned. What was he supposed to say to Oliver? And why was Parker mentioning him? They hadn't even met before. He'd always kept his New York life and his California life separated because he didn't feel like New York Matt and California Matt were the same person.

"Eh. I just figured you would have spoken to him. You talk to him more than you do anyone else. If I were the jealous type, I might have disliked him on principle."

That was a surprise. He would have never expected to hear Parker say he could be envious of Ollie…but he did know he felt more comfortable talking to Oliver than anyone else. On the flip side, Parker had seen sides of him Oliver never would. Things Oliver wouldn't understand because he was so goddamned perfect and Matt would always be flawed.

Still…he missed him. Hearing Parker mention Oliver made Matt miss him more. "There would never be a reason to be jealous of Ollie. He's my best friend and that's all. We're too different." Oliver had always felt a responsibility toward Matt. He knew that. How could he not? He'd known Matt as the kid whose mom worked for his family. Then the kid who liked to play the piano but never had money for lessons. The kid who Oliver begged his parents to sponsor so he could go to an arts high school Matt could never have gotten into on his own.

He appreciated what Oliver did for him, and he always would, but there was no reason to be jealous. "This isn't about Oliver," Matt added, hoping that would take Oliver from his thoughts. "What are we going to do about work?"

"There's nothing to do. You're my client if you want to be. You know that, Matt. We're friends outside of our careers, but you're not working anyway. You're making excuses not to work. I think you need to ask yourself why. Take some time—get your thoughts in order; figure out what you want."

What the hell would he do? Before he was modeling, he'd worked three dead-end jobs trying to make ends meet. He'd never gone to school like he planned. He'd eventually stopped trying to compose because nothing ever came of it. He didn't play anymore. Sad as it was, modeling was all he had. "It's my career. What choice do I have?"

Parker winked at him and grinned. "There's always a choice, baby boy. Think about it. Get out of the city. Go home. See your friends. Do something. You're too fucking pretty to look so damn sad." Parker stood. "I'm going to bed. I'll see you in a bit."

With a shrug, he walked from the room but his words were still with Matt. *Go home. See your friends. You're too fucking pretty.*

It always came down to that. When he'd left LA, he'd sworn he would find a way to make something of himself on his own, without any help from Oliver. Without relying on people desiring him physically for him to get ahead…but he hadn't done that, had he? And that was part of the reason it felt tarnished. Part of the reason the emptiness inside him continued to grow. Beneath the surface, he was still that same kid he'd always been.

Matt hated it when he had to go with his mom to work. It was such bullshit. He always felt out of place in that house. Oliver would try to talk to him because he felt sorry for him. His friends Chance and Miles sort of hung around in the background like they wondered what Oliver was doing. He was rich. His life was perfect. He was already out of the closet, and his mom and dad were like Gay Crusader parents when Matt's own looked at him like he was an alien from another planet. They were confused by him…didn't understand him.

Oliver's family was like the perfect families you saw on TV.

And Matt had to spend his summer days helping his mom clean their house. Fucking great. It was torture because when he did come, he just wanted to play. To sit at Oliver's piano and pretend it was his, which only annoyed him, especially when Oliver was around and didn't seem to realize how cool the instrument was.

Luckily, Oliver's parents were out of town and he was spending the week at his friend Chance's house—at least that was what Matt's mom had told him.

Tired of having to help his mom with things he didn't want to do, Matt made his way into their living room.

It was kind of ridiculous. Nothing was out of place. The carpets were a cream color and there wasn't a single stain on them. But then he thought maybe he was cutting them a raw deal too because despite how perfect it was…their house was also homey. Comfortable. They had family pictures all over the walls and an award Oliver won for an essay-writing contest. Their house was filled with memories and happiness, and Matt was in such a shitty mood that it annoyed him even more.

In a bad enough mood to let his eyes find the expensive piano in the corner of the room that taunted him every time he came over.

Since no one was here other than his mom who was cleaning upstairs, he let himself walk over to it. Let his fingers feel the cool, white and black keys. Imagined that it was his. That he could play it any time he wanted. That he took lessons and there was an award on the wall he'd won for playing.

And then he sat down on the bench…put his fingers on the keys…and began to play.

He had a keyboard at home that he'd gotten for Christmas, but it was nothing like this. The clear sound wasn't the same, and it didn't feel the same. This was life. It was passion and energy and happiness all wrapped up in one.

He played a song he'd written himself, something he taught himself on his keyboard that he pretended he'd never have to play again. Because this was his piano in his house, and he could let the music that lived inside of him out any moment he wanted to.

"Matt! What are you doing? That's expensive! You can't mess around with other people's things."

He tried to ignore his mom's voice, tried to keep playing but then someone else spoke. "It's okay, ma'am. He can play it. He's not going to *hurt anything."*

Matt froze at the sound of Oliver's voice. His cheeks heated at the thought of Oliver having heard him play and his mom scolding him for it.

"Thank you, Oliver. That was nice of him, wasn't it, Matt?" his mom asked.

Matt closed his eyes, took a deep breath, ignored the part of him that just wanted to walk out, and turned to Oliver. "Yeah. Thanks. I appreciate it."

Oliver waved his hand. "It's not a big deal. It's just a piano."

Just a piano? Just a fucking piano? Matt clenched his fists.

"You're awesome. Like, extremely good. I didn't know you played," Oliver told him.

When Matt didn't reply, his mom said, "Oh, he just plays around. He is very good, though."

But it wasn't just playing around to Matt. It was his dream. They didn't understand that.

His mom spoke to Oliver some more. Apparently, his parents were returning early and would be there in a few hours. His friend Chance's mom had dropped him off.

"Do you want to come up to my room and play some video games with me?" Oliver asked him.

Matt's eyes shot to his mom, and he hoped she wouldn't say that he had to help her clean. Thankfully, she gave him a small smile and a quick nod.

"Or you can keep playing the piano if you want. What else can you play?" Oliver asked.

As much as Matt thought about playing in front of people, that wasn't his thing. He felt too "on display" when people watched him so he shook his head. "Nah, I'm done here. What games do you have?" he asked.

Oliver led him upstairs, telling him all the games he had. They played for an hour, and he realized Oliver wasn't a douchebag like Matt thought he would be. Oliver was nice.

When Matt had to leave, Oliver said maybe he could come with his mom next time and play the piano and some more video games with him, and Matt realized how much he wanted that.

From that day forward, Oliver was his best friend.

Matt's eyes popped open from his dream. He didn't know how long he'd slept, likely not long since it was still dark outside, but he knew Parker was right. He needed to go home. He needed to take a break and figure out what in the hell was going on with him.

CHAPTER THREE

THEY STAYED UNTIL Wild Side closed. It wasn't often they made it until two but with Chance dancing and the drinks readily flowing, Oliver's head spun in a way it hadn't for years. He'd drank too much, way too fucking much. He couldn't control his laughter as he stumbled out of the bar, Miles and Chance on either side of him. He had an arm wrapped around each of the men and could feel the goofy-ass smile on his face.

Life was pretty fucking good. He had two of his best friends by his side, and yeah, if he was being honest, Eddie wasn't so bad. He might have exaggerated the nasal sound just a bit. The man was gorgeous and seemed to like Oliver, so what did he have to lose?

"I'm definitely going to fuck Eddie tomorrow night. It's been too long since I've gotten any ass." Jesus, he missed sex. Why didn't he fuck more often? Why did he always have to care about feelings and knowing someone? Why couldn't it just be about orgasms and blowjobs?

Chance let out a loud laugh, and Oliver knew if he looked at Miles, his friend would be shaking his head at him.

"Skipping head and going straight to fucking. This is very serious for you," Miles replied.

Chance said, "I'm in agreement. You don't have enough sex. I've said that for years." They stopped on the busy corner of Sunset Boulevard. From the corner of his eye, Oliver could see the familiar sign with the silver "W" and *Wild* to the left and *Side* to the right of it. All the bars and clubs were emptying out, the sidewalks flooded with people. Chance wiped the smeared eyeliner from beneath his eyes with his finger, the nail painted pink.

"Oh yeah. You had a good time." A sexy guy with a shaved head smiled at Oliver, obviously clued into his drunkenness.

"Thanks for noticing," Oliver replied with a grin, and both Miles and Chance laughed from beside him. He loved this. Spending time with his friends. He wished Matt was here with them, but he was lucky to have Chance and Miles.

They stood at the corner for a moment and Chance commented, "You must really like nose guy. You don't fuck just anyone, Mr. Romance."

It wasn't that he thought he loved the guy or anything. He was horny; Eddie was nice and good-looking. Oliver deserved an orgasm from someone other than his own hand and too much porn—if there was such a thing as too much porn.

"Or he's just drunk, and he'll change his mind tomorrow." Miles tried to burst his bubble. It was a knack he had.

Oliver rolled his eyes. He wasn't going to let Miles kill his buzz. "I'm getting a car." He pulled out his phone and noticed five missed calls from Matt. His pulse automatically started to sprint.

"What is it?" Miles asked and tried to look over his shoulder at his phone. He was good at reading Oliver. Miles was good at reading most people.

"Matt. He called five times. It's late for him. Something must be up." Plus, it had been a while since he'd heard from him. He didn't say that, though. Verbalizing it would just get Miles going and make it so Chance had to play peacekeeper.

"Here we go." Miles rolled his eyes.

"What the fuck? He's our friend, man." Just as Oliver went to dial Matt back, his phone rang again. "Hello?" he answered, his heartbeat doing the fifty-yard dash over and over. What had Matty in such a hurry to get ahold of him?

"Hey. I've been trying to call you all night. Where have you been?" Matt's voice was soft, a little sad, and he would swear, almost unsure. He hadn't heard that tone from him in years.

"I was out with Chance and Miles. What's wrong?" He paced back and forth, one hand in his pocket, the other clutching the phone. Both Miles and Chance eyed him expectantly as Oliver tried to fight the twist in his gut, his buzz disappearing fast.

"How do you know something's wrong?"

How could he not know? That was what friends were for, what they did, especially one who'd known someone as long as he'd known Matt. What he said was, "You called five times and it's late." Short. Simple. To the point.

Matt chuckled, but Oliver could tell it was forced. He didn't want Oliver to know something was wrong. *And, I need to stop trying to read Matt's mind.*

"I guess that makes sense. Are you still with the crew?" Matty asked.

He looked up and locked eyes with Chance and Miles. They were both staring intensely at him, nearly bursting at the seams to know what was going on. "They just left. I'm waiting for my car," he lied. Maybe that made him an ass but he was nervous that if he didn't, Matty wouldn't talk to him.

Miles rolled his eyes but Oliver ignored him.

Matt let out a deep breath. "What's wrong, Matty?" Oliver asked again before he leaned against the black building with peeling paint.

"Parker and I broke up."

Oliver closed his eyes, trying to block out the lively city around him. "I'm sorry," he told Matt, and he was. The last thing he would ever want was for Matt to be hurt.

"I just…fuck, I don't know. I need to get away, to clear my

head. I'm at the airport now. I'll be in LA in the morning. I know it's last minute, but can I stay with you?"

It wasn't as though Matt didn't have the money to get a room. Staying with his family wasn't something Matt would do. Oliver knew that. They were good people, but Matt always had a strange relationship with them. They loved Matt and Matt loved them, but they didn't understand each other. It made things awkward between them, something that just got worse the older Matt grew.

"Shit, I don't know why I asked you that. It's not your responsibility to put me up. There's no reason I can't get a room—not anymore."

But why should he have to? Oliver had space. He opened his eyes and looked at his two friends, knowing they would get the wrong idea about his answer. "That's ridiculous. It'll be like old times. You know you're always welcome to stay with me."

He watched as Miles shook his head and Chance frowned. What? They wouldn't let Matt stay with them if he needed to? They might worry about Oliver when it came to Matt, but they cared about him too. Both of his friends standing in front of him would let Matt stay with them if he needed a place to go. There was no difference.

"Shit." Matt cursed softly through the line, but Oliver wasn't sure why. Then he added, "Thank you. I appreciate it, Ollie. I'm about to board. Can you not say anything to Chance and Miles just yet? I think I just need to breathe for a day or two before I see anyone else."

Oliver locked eyes with the men in question. *A little late for that.* "No problem. I won't say anything to them." He cocked a brow at his friends. Miles threw his hands up in the air as though he didn't know what to do with him, and Chance grinned, obviously liking being in on a secret he wasn't supposed to be in on.

"Thank you. I land a little after eight. I can get a car—"

"I'll pick you up. You can worry about a car later." Oliver cut him off. He couldn't bring himself to look at Miles because he knew he'd get the evil eye.

"Yeah, okay. I need to go. I'll…I'll see you soon."

He could hear the denial in Matt's voice, hear him trying to hold back the emotion because Matt wasn't big on letting people know how he felt…but he had to be struggling. He'd just broken up with the man he loved, and Matt was obviously devastated. "Bye, Matty. I'm sorry about you and Parker."

"It's okay," he said and then, "talk soon," before he hung up. The second Oliver moved the phone away from his ear, Miles started in.

"He and his boyfriend broke up, he called you, and now he's coming here?"

"Don't make it sound like that. He's not coming to see me specifically because his relationship ended. He needs to get away and this is home. Oh, and he doesn't want you guys to know, so don't say anything."

Chance answered with, "I guess you're not getting head from the guy with postnasal drip. Maybe that's for the best. It could have gotten messy."

Oliver wanted to laugh but he couldn't. He didn't know what he felt right now. All he knew was, he wished he could have another drink.

CHAPTER FOUR

OLIVER DIDN'T SLEEP all night. He tried for a couple of hours, then got up and worked out and drank coffee before it was time to leave for the airport.

He'd texted Matt to let him know he'd wait outside at baggage claim.

He wasn't going inside, and he didn't stop to get Matt a coffee. See? He wasn't at Matt's beck and call anymore. He knew that was what Miles thought and probably Chance too, only Chance would beat around the bush and joke about it where Miles would give him the cold shoulder or straight up call him out on it.

That was the thing with being friends with the same people all your life. No one knew him better than his friends and he knew them equally well. It made it difficult to get away with any shit.

This time they were wrong.

Oliver decided he wasn't calling off his date tonight. LA was home for Matt. He could hang out around Oliver's place or keep himself busy while Oliver went out. It wasn't as if he wouldn't be able to find things to do. It also wasn't as if he didn't have parents here who would want to see him either.

LAX was a mess like it always was—traffic was bumper to bumper. People were everywhere, flagging cabs and jumping into vehicles, honking and screaming at each other. As frustrating as it was, that was LA and he was not only used to it, he loved it.

It was over half an hour after Matt's flight landed when Oliver saw him come outside. He stuck out in the crowd making its way through the doors. He looked good as always—tall and lean. Maybe a little too skinny, but then Matt had always been thin. Still, Oliver could see defined, sinewy muscles running the lengths of his arms. He wore what was obviously a high-priced T-shirt and jeans. His dark hair was styled shorter on the sides and longer on top. It stood up like he'd run his hands through it, but Oliver knew that was exactly how Matt wanted it to look. If not, it would hang in his eyes, which Oliver had always thought was sexy as hell.

A frown curved Matt's lips. He had a light dusting of hair on his jaw that looked like it had been cut from stone...but somehow delicately. That was Matt, delicately masculine features. It obviously did it for Oliver.

He jumped when there was a honk behind him. *Fuck.* He was holding up traffic staring at Matt. This wasn't a good sign. He stuck his hand out the window and flipped off whoever was being impatient before the car just drove around him. Oliver pulled up to the curb and jumped out of his car.

Matty slipped his sunglasses off, looked over at Oliver and grinned. The dimple under the right side of his mouth didn't look quite as deep as it did when Matt truly smiled but still, it was a sexy-as-hell smile.

His teeth were perfectly white and straight—they always had been. His family never would've been able to afford braces—he hadn't worn them, but you'd think he had. Oliver had worn them for three years and his teeth were nothing like Matt's.

"Hey, buddy. What's up?" Matt said after walking over. Another car honked followed by a second loud blast.

"Hey." Oliver gave him a one-armed hug. "Let's get your stuff in the trunk and get out of here before I get into a fight with somcone." They likely weren't honking at them. There were cars everywhere, but Oliver still wanted to get the fuck on the road.

He opened the trunk, and Matt put his bags inside. Less than a minute later, they were in the car and trying to get through the mass of traffic.

"How was your flight?" Oliver asked, looking over his shoulder and trying to make his way out.

"It was a flight."

Without looking, he knew Matt had shrugged.

"Thanks for picking me up. I should have just gotten a car. I don't know why I didn't. I'm going to need one to get around."

Before, Oliver used to pick him up because they didn't have a choice. Matt couldn't afford a car. Sure, he could have taken a cab, but Oliver had always just wanted to pick him up. Now, Matt didn't need him to do that. Still, he liked that his old friend kept their familiar routine. It made him feel like the guy sitting next to him was the same Matt he'd always known, even though he hadn't seen him in a few years. "You know it's no problem."

Matt leaned his head against the seat and closed his eyes. They were quiet the whole way to Oliver's house in Laurel Canyon. He'd always known he'd want to live outside of the city, somewhere more secluded. He loved the pulse of life, the business of LA and Hollywood, but when he was at home he wanted to be away from it all.

As soon as they pulled into his driveway, Matt stirred. He sat up and looked at Oliver's house and the land it sat on. He had a white, two-story home. It was nestled in trees on a hill. If Matt went out back, he would see a view of the city skyline, his pool surrounded by rock. "Jesus, it's beautiful, Ollie."

It was big—too much for one person, really, but it was Oliver's oasis. He loved writing out by the pool or taking in the view from his office.

"Thank you," he replied as Matt's words hit him. He'd lived here two years and Matt had never seen it. Things like that were still strange to him. They'd been so close for so many years. It didn't seem possible that he could live somewhere for two years that Matt hadn't seen in person.

But then, he'd never been out to New York to see Matt. How could that be the case? He didn't understand the way the distance between them had grown since Matt left.

They got out of his car and went around back to the trunk. Oliver grabbed a bag, Matt the other before he led his friend into the house.

The entryway was open, with a white bench against the wall Oliver had found at a yard sale. Some of the paint was peeling, but that gave it the charm he loved. "Do you want a tour now or later?" He figured he would give Matt a choice. He'd been awake and flying all night. The last thing Matt likely wanted was to walk around Oliver's house.

"Later, if you don't mind."

"No problem. Just an FYI—living room is that way." Oliver pointed to the left. "Kitchen that way." Then the right. "Dining room is behind it. The hallway to the side of the stairs leads to my office and another bathroom. That way if you come down while I'm writing, you know where to go."

Oliver went toward the stairs and led him up to the room Matt would be staying in. There were three rooms upstairs and one down by his office. He opened the door to Matt's. "You have your own bath. The balcony looks out over the hills. It's on the wrong side for the view of the city. You'd have to stay in my room for that." Oliver winked at him and Matt rolled his eyes.

"Selfish. Always keeping the best shit for yourself."

The two of them laughed briefly before silence took over. Matt didn't look at him, but Oliver couldn't look anywhere else. Matt was hurting. Oliver could see the pain in the slump of his shoulders, the dullness in his light green eyes. They were always so vivid but right now the color was muted, foggy with a deep ache that Oliver understood. It hurt to lose someone you loved. Even though Matt had never been his, that was how he imagined he looked when Matty left.

"You seem tired," Oliver told him.

Matt nodded, running a hand through his hair. "Yeah…I am. I figured I'd take a nap if you don't mind." Oliver frowned and Matt said, "Okay, I knew you wouldn't mind."

And then they stood there without moving. Things were awkward for them, and he really fucking hated that awkwardness. It had never been there between them, not since they became friends, not even when Oliver was mentally obsessing over Matt as a kid.

Oliver could walk away. To anyone else he probably should walk away. Matt was tired, and he wouldn't be able to fall asleep very well with Oliver standing in his doorway like the creepy stalker he was afraid he was starting to become. But he didn't move, just waited for what he figured would come. What he knew would come if things were the same between them as they used to be.

And Jesus, he fucking hoped things were the same. He could handle a lot of things but losing the bond and friendship he'd always had with Matty wasn't one of them.

Finally, Matt let go of his bag, stepped closer, and wrapped his arms around Oliver. Oliver returned the hug, breathed him in, the mixture of coffee and cologne. He wanted the spicy scent of the cologne gone. It wasn't Matt—not the Matt he knew—but it had become the Matt on billboards for cologne. His Matt carried nothing but his own scent on his skin—that somehow smelled like music on paper. "I feel like my whole fucking life is falling apart."

Oliver cupped the back of Matt's head, feeling his soft hair, rougher because of the product in it. "I know, babe." It was nothing for Oliver to call him that. He used to do it all the time, but he felt Matt's muscles briefly go taut before relaxing again.

This was Matt letting his guard down. Oliver knew he needed to, knew he would. He also knew it wouldn't last. Matt was never good at being vulnerable. He'd briefly let cracks show in his armor before he welded them shut again.

Just as predicted, a short moment later, Matt pulled back.

"Did you guys try to make it work? You and Parker?" Oliver asked. "Maybe there's a chance." If Matt was this broken up about it, he obviously still loved his ex.

"No." There was a finality to Matt's voice. It was there, in the bones of his voice, the fact that he and Parker were really over. "It was long overdue. Toward the end, he was with other men more than he was with me, and I found that I didn't care. I almost felt relief. My head hasn't been in the right place for a while."

Oliver's blood went cold, ice crystallizing his veins. "He cheated on you?" *What a piece of shit.* That was something Oliver would never understand. He could never be with someone and betray them like that. He just didn't get why people stepped on the feelings of others so easily.

"No," Matt replied softly. "I knew about it. We had rules in place. It worked for us. I played too, Ollie, a lot more in the beginning. And sometimes Parker and I played together with other people."

The twist in Oliver's gut coiled tighter, crawled into his chest and through his throat. Jesus, Matt and Parker had been together for years. They lived together, but they fucked and played with other men both together and separately? Was that the kind of relationship he wanted?

Oliver didn't move. Hell, he wasn't sure if he was breathing right then. He just stood there looking at the man standing in front of him. He'd been fascinated with Matt since the first time he came home and caught Matt playing his piano. If he were being honest, he'd wanted to know more about Matt even before that.

But standing there in that moment was the first time he really understood, truly felt that there was no chance he and Matt would've ever been good together. They were too different, wanted different things. They were an impossibility.

Oliver had no problem with people living their lives how they wanted. Want an open relationship? Go for it. Fuck your way through life? Have at it. As long as you were happy, that was all that mattered, so he didn't look down at Matt because of how he'd lived his life with Parker, but he knew that couldn't be him. It would never be him. There wasn't a chance he'd ever share someone he thought he loved.

And he also didn't know what to say right now.

Matt spoke before he had the chance. "Don't do that. Please don't fucking do that. Don't judge me, Oliver."

"I'm not." But they both knew he kind of was.

"I can see it in your face. Different doesn't mean wrong."

"Fuck." Oliver cursed quietly because Matt was right. He knew that, but he wasn't acting like it. "You're right. To each their own. I meant no disrespect." Hell, Matt was the only one out of the two of them who'd had a long-term relationship. Maybe he knew something Oliver didn't.

Matt sighed, but a small smile teased his lips. "I know you didn't." He reached out, grabbed the front of Oliver's shirt so that his hand was against Oliver's stomach. "Big-hearted Oliver Hayes. You're too kind for something like that." He tugged Oliver's shirt playfully and then let go. "I'm going to lie down." He disappeared behind the door into Oliver's guest room. Oliver stood there for a moment, thinking about Matt….How different he seemed…how lost, before he forced himself to go downstairs and write. He needed to stop overthinking everything where Matt was concerned and wondering what happened to the boy he'd known.

CHAPTER FIVE

IT WAS TOO quiet for Matt to sleep. He'd known Oliver lived out in the hills of Laurel Canyon, but he didn't realize how silent it would actually be. He was too used to New York City where people never slept. There were always lights and sounds and an energy he kept expecting but didn't receive.

Or hell, maybe he was using that as an excuse, and it was really the combination of what went down with Parker added to the way Oliver had looked at him when he'd shared the details about their relationship.

He wasn't ashamed of the decision they'd made together. He also wasn't surprised by Oliver's reaction to it. He and Oliver had always seen a lot of things differently. Hell, it was like they lived on different planets sometimes. Oliver would always do things the right way, and Matt would usually do them the wrong way. Oliver was kind and Matt was gruff. Oliver would always accomplish whatever he set his mind to; Matt gave up. It was just how they were built.

But he also knew that in reality Oliver hadn't meant any harm by it. He wasn't the kind of man to purposely look down on someone or to judge them…but that didn't mean he didn't do it sometimes. He held the world to his standard without realizing he did it, and most people just couldn't be who Ollie was.

So he continued to lie in the bed that felt a little too soft. The room was beautiful. Everything was white from the crisp, clean walls to the accent tables and the bedding.

The house was perfect for Oliver. It was exactly what he saw the man having. He'd always known Oliver would make something of himself. It was sewn into his DNA.

For a moment, Matt wondered what Oliver thought of him, of his career. Was he proud of Matt? He'd always said he was, but did he really mean it? Or was there a part of Oliver that thought Matt had failed since he wasn't composing music? Because that would be the truth.

"Fuck," Matt gritted out, annoyed at himself for going there. Getting away from the shit that clogged up his mind was the whole point of leaving New York, but then he'd never been very good at letting things go.

His stomach growled, but he ignored it and rolled over in the bed. He'd opened the curtains before lying down. He saw trees instead of buildings. The wind blew, and he watched the leaves rustle in it. He felt a world away from New York or even LA, but then he figured that was why Ollie lived out here. He probably locked himself in his office for hours on end while he wrote.

It was all Oliver had ever wanted to do, and even though there was the twinge of jealousy deep in his gut, Matt smiled because Oliver was living the life he'd always wanted. If anyone deserved that, it was Ollie.

MATT'S EYES OPENED slowly, and he realized he'd managed to get some sleep.

A lot of it.

He hadn't expected that. The sun looked as though it was already starting to go down. He stretched, grabbed his phone off the nightstand and shot a quick text to Parker, letting him know everything was okay. He likely wouldn't get a reply, which was fine. Parker was a man of few words when it came to shit like that.

He set his phone back down and went into the en suite where he took a quick piss, washed his hands and then splashed water on his face.

He had bags under his eyes that Parker would give him shit over if he saw them.

Matt went back into the bedroom and thought about making a quick call to his parents. He got an uncomfortable twist in his abdomen and decided before he did anything, he needed to clean up.

He took a shower. The hot water felt so fucking good he could have come from it. Then he climbed out, brushed his teeth, and got dressed.

Matt pulled out his laptop and turned it on. He had emails from Parker, work shit and too many things he didn't want to deal with. Work shit he needed to find a way to deal with before there wasn't any work shit left—then he'd really be fucked.

Christ, what was he doing to himself? The whole point had been to come home and get away.

He gave his phone another glance but hell, it was already late in the day. It wasn't like he would go see them this evening. Maybe he and Ollie could hang out—watch a movie or something.

The more he thought about that the more some of the tightness gripping his muscles seemed to ease up. Maybe they could go out or have a drink or...fuck, he didn't know, something. Oliver had always made things feel better, and right now, Matt really fucking needed that.

Ignoring his phone and his laptop, he made his way downstairs.

He went to turn into the living room but somehow knew that Ollie wasn't there.

As he went down the hall, he heard a familiar sound that made him stop, a smile stretching across his face.

Jesus, his friend was crazy. He didn't know why he was surprised but he was. Maybe it was because he felt like such a different person from the man he'd been when he left LA that he assumed Oliver would be too.

He rapped softly on the door, before hearing a quiet, "Come in."

The second he had the door open he said, "Sounds of the rainforest? Still?"

Oliver looked up from behind his desk, a computer in front of him. "It helps me write. If it ain't broke, don't fix it."

Chuckling, Matt stepped into the room. "Yeah, I guess you have a point there."

Oliver's office was decorated in rich earth tones—browns and greens.

He had a large dark wood L-shaped desk that was of course, immaculate, with everything in its place.

The curtains were open. There was a standing lamp in one corner of the room and another small lamp on his desk. Across from where he sat were two chairs with a small table between them. And behind him…

"Holy fuck, Ollie."

Matt walked over, slipping past his friend to study the wall behind him. It was full of picture after picture. Oliver and Chance. Oliver and Miles. Miles and Chance. Oliver, Miles, Chance, and himself—birthday parties and graduations. School plays and Ollie, Miles, and Chance's trip to Europe in high school.

Their whole lives were on this wall, years and years of friendship and memories and good times.…And in the middle was a picture of Oliver and himself. Ollie had his arm around Matt, with a smile so fucking bright it shined like the sun.

And Matt was smiling just as happily.

He wanted that.

Missed that.

Needed to find a way to feel that happiness again because he'd lost it. He didn't know how or why or hell, maybe he'd never really had it, but at different points in his life, he'd felt like he did. In this picture, Matt saw a tease of it and couldn't remember the last time he'd felt it.

Pure, raw, real happiness.

"This is incredible," he told Oliver, who stood up and moved to stand beside him.

"We're lucky…the friendship the four of us have. Not everyone is blessed with that."

No, no they weren't. If it hadn't been for Oliver, Matt wouldn't have had it.

"I can't look back at my life without remembering something that involves you, Chance, or Miles. I wouldn't be the person I am without you guys."

Oliver scoffed at that. "I highly doubt that. You don't give yourself enough credit."

"Somehow, I don't think I'm the only one who does that."

He glanced over to see Oliver cock a dark brow at him.

"It helps me write," Ollie admitted as they stood there looking at the wall. Matt couldn't take his eyes off the center picture of the two of them. "I draw a lot from real-life experiences or the people I know.…Or hell, maybe it's just you guys that keep me grounded to reality, so I don't lose myself in the worlds I create where I always get to decide what happens."

"Oh, fuck. I should have been a writer," Matt teased. Then he could write his own reality where he made a life doing what he loved.

Right now though, he just wanted this—what he saw on the wall. Wanted to laugh and talk and just fucking *be* without letting all the other shit drag him down. "Can we hang out tonight?" Matt asked. "I don't care what we do, just something."

"Oh," Oliver replied softly from beside him. "I can't. I have a date tonight."

A burst of surprise went off inside Matt. He didn't know why. It made sense that Oliver would be dating. Hell, it didn't make sense that Matt had been in a long-term relationship and Oliver hadn't. He should have a partner in his house with him, someone who loved the same way Ollie did.

"I would cancel but—"

"What? Shut up. Why should you cancel? I'm a big boy. I'll be okay on my own." He tried to ignore the twinge of disappointment that he couldn't spend his first night back in Los Angeles with Oliver. But then, maybe Ollie had felt the same way when Matt canceled trips or came into town for a quick shoot and hadn't had time to see his friends.

"I don't have to leave for about an hour. Want to go into the kitchen with me? I'll see what I can find for you to eat. You have to be hungry. You haven't eaten all day."

Matt shook his head. Oliver likely needed to get ready for his date. He didn't want Oliver to feel as though he had to babysit him.

"No, I'm not hungry. I'll grab something later. I should call Parker and take care of a few things."

"Okay," he replied.

Matt nudged him. "Have fun on your date. Get laid for me," he teased and then made his way out of Oliver's office, trying to ignore the growing disappointment taking root inside of him.

CHAPTER SIX

I T HAD BEEN hell leaving Matt at home.

Oliver could tell he'd been hurt but tried to cover it. He'd wanted to stay just because of that. It was important for him to try and make people feel better—Matt especially—but on the other hand, Miles was right. He needed to start thinking about himself as well, and there was no reason he should have to cancel his date because Matty came home at the last minute.

Even if his date did have the worst case of allergies Oliver had ever seen.

Eddie lived in Hollywood, so the drive wasn't too long. This was the first time he'd been to Eddie's apartment since they'd started dating. They usually met wherever they were going.

He was a graphic designer. He lived in a nice building where Oliver actually found parking, which was a plus.

When he turned off the car, part of him wanted to turn it right back on and drive away.

He's attractive…and nice…and I'm horny, he told himself and tried not to think about Matty at all. About the way his voice had lowered when he'd realized Oliver was going out or the light he saw in Matt's eyes as he took in the pictures—the light he hadn't seen in too damn long.

He looked at the address again on his phone to get Eddie's apartment number. Oliver made his way to the building; the closer he got, the more he knew he'd made the right decision in coming.

See? Miles was wrong. He could go out and fuck when he wanted to. He wasn't living in some fantasy world where he was sitting around and waiting for Matt. He was going to have a nice, quiet evening alone with a sexy man followed by a much-needed orgasm.

When Oliver got to apartment B12 he held up his fist and rapped on the door. It was only a few seconds later that he heard the locks turning and then…

"Hi. Oh. You're not Eddie."

The other man smiled. "Hi. I'm the roommate, Mike. Nice to meet you." He held out his hand and Oliver shook it.

"You as well."

Mike let him into the apartment. A dull annoyance tugged at Oliver, but he tried to ignore it. Why did it matter if Mike was here? It wasn't like he should have to leave just because Eddie had a date over.

"Eddie's in the kitchen," Mike told him. They went through the living room which led into the small open-concept kitchen and dining room. Eddie stood at the stove mixing something in a pan.

He turned, his blue eyes bright and wide. "Hey. It's good to see you." Eddie walked over and gave him a hug. "Do you want some wine?"

"Sure," Oliver replied before leaning against the counter as Eddie went back to the stove.

Mike grabbed a bottle, uncorked it, and pulled three wine glasses down.

They drank and the three of them talked while Eddie continued to cook. As time went on Oliver began feeling more and more ridiculous. It was obvious he'd been wrong about this date and what Eddie was looking for. Did he think Eddie would have sex with him if he wanted? Yeah, it was likely, but Oliver had been making excuses not to go out with him when it looked like Eddie might only be looking for a friend, anyway.

Story of his life.

When dinner was done, the three of them sat down to eat together. Eddie had made spaghetti and meatballs, which were good.

The three of them continued talking and laughing. Eddie and Mike kept the wine going, but Oliver cut himself off. He had never been much of a wine drinker. He could handle a glass or two but it stopped there. As the evening went on, he actually enjoyed the man's company more than he'd expected. Which of course, made sense considering he was pretty sure Eddie wasn't any more interested in Oliver than Oliver had thought he was interested in Eddie.

When they finished eating, they cleared the table. He and Eddie went to the couch to watch a movie and Mike excused himself to his bedroom.

They weren't very far into the comedy before Eddie's hand went to the back of his neck, his fingers running through Oliver's light brown hair. "You look gorgeous tonight."

Huh. Maybe he was wrong in his worry about tonight? Which was confusing even in his own head. "Thank you. So do you."

He turned toward Eddie just as the other man's lips came down on his. Oliver let Eddie kiss him, kissed him back but damned if he didn't start thinking about postnasal drip, and visions of all the things Miles and Chance teased him about played like a movie in his brain.

It was a reflex to jerk back. Eddie's eyes went wide. "What's wrong?" he asked.

Jesus, Oliver. Get it the fuck together. You're acting like a child. "Nothing." Oliver smiled at him. "Come here," he said, and Eddie leaned forward again.

Their lips had just touched when the fucking movie started in his head again and he imagined Eddie's gurgle laugh in his ear and he really didn't want the man's tongue in his mouth.

As though Eddie heard him, he began to kiss his way down Oliver's throat. "Your skin tastes good," he said. "Do you want to go into the bedroom with me?"

No, he thought but instead said, "Yes." Because it was sex and an orgasm, and it had been a long-ass time for him.

Plus, he wanted to prove to Miles and to himself he could hook up, and it didn't matter if Matt was here or not.

Eddie kissed his throat again. "Do you mind if Mike joins us?" he whispered against Oliver's flesh.

He froze. "Excuse me?"

"Just for fun," Eddie clarified. "Sometimes we like to have threesomes with our dates, but it's okay if you aren't interested."

"What?"

"Threesome. Like I said, it's okay if—"

"No. I heard you. I'm just wondering what I said or did that made you think I would want to have a threesome with you and your roommate the first time I've even slept with you?" *Was this a thing? Unplanned threesomes?*

"What?" Eddie asked as though he didn't understand Oliver's hesitance. And maybe he didn't. Maybe this was another way Oliver was different from most of the people he knew.

"You don't just do that. It's different if you meet someone at a bar or something and ask them if they want to come home with you for a threesome, but you don't ask that of someone you've dated who has never once given you any inclination that they'd want to fuck you and your roommate. Jesus." This time when he pulled back, he planned to stay there.

And then it happened…Eddie gave an uncomfortable laugh, and there was the gurgle that made Oliver want to lose his dinner.

"Oh, fuck. I need to get out of here." He stood and Eddie did as well. Oliver began walking away before Eddie spoke again.

"It was just a question. You don't have to be so uptight."

He stopped and turned. "I know it was. And maybe I am too uptight." His friends would likely think he was. "I don't want to fuck you and your roommate. There are probably plenty of men out there that do, though. I suggest looking into Grindr for a hookup."

Without another word, Oliver left the apartment. He couldn't write this shit if he tried.

CHAPTER SEVEN

MATT SAT ON Oliver's couch feeling antsy. Oliver had left a couple of hours before to go on his date. He found himself wondering about the man Oliver was going out with. Had they been dating long? What was he like? Why hadn't Matt heard about him earlier? Were they serious? It surprised him that Oliver hadn't had a serious relationship before. He would never have thought he'd have been the one in a relationship before Oliver, but then in some people's eyes maybe what he and Parker had didn't qualify, and it was over anyway.

It was something he'd always expected from Oliver, though. He deserved a good man like himself and Matt couldn't help but wonder if he'd found that in the guy he was seeing tonight.

Matt let his eyes wander to the corner of the room—to the piano that looked as it had the first time Matt saw it in Oliver's house as a child. He'd been drawn to it right away. Wanted nothing more than to run his fingers over the white and black keys.

Seeing it again made him feel like that boy with his dream right in front of his fingertips but not able to grasp it. Made him remember what it was like to see Oliver who had all the things Matt didn't have but was also so damn nice that he kept asking Matt if he wanted to hang out with him and his friends, no matter how many times he said no.

Before that day with the piano, he'd always turned him down, even though he'd wanted nothing more than to be friends with

Oliver.

"Fuck." Matt shook his head and shoved to his feet, annoyed at himself for being such a mopey bastard. He'd been back in LA for less than twenty-four hours, and he was already starting to feel sorry for himself.

His stomach let out a deep growl, so he ignored the piano in the room and made his way toward Oliver's kitchen. He couldn't remember the last time he'd eaten something.

The kitchen was a spacious room with high-end appliances and somehow had a modern yet rustic feel at the same time. It fit Oliver perfectly.

Matt's stomach rumbled again, so he opened Oliver's pantry and looked at the expansive space. "Jesus fucking Christ, Ollie. I could live in here," he mumbled to himself. He didn't know why it was a surprise to him. It was similar to the pantry Oliver had in his childhood home, which had been about the size of Matt's bedroom.

The shelves were perfectly organized—snacks, baking supplies, dinner foods, all separated into their own section—and Matt found himself chuckling. Some things never changed. Oliver had always been somewhat of a perfectionist, and he loved knowing his friend still had those tendencies.

He shuffled things around looking for something that he knew Oliver always had on hand. Matt pushed boxes and packages to the side, knowing that it had to be here somewhere. It took him a moment to realize he was frowning. It was stupid to feel…almost hurt. People grew, their taste buds changed; he was looking for a box of cereal for fuck's sake, but then he saw it—two boxes to be exact, shoved behind pancake mix—chocolate and regular Lucky Charms.

His lips pulled into a smile. Matt grabbed both boxes and set them on the bar. Christ, he hadn't let himself indulge in his favorite cereal for so long. *Damn it.* He deserved this. He'd just had a breakup. He could eat bad shit for at least one day.

It took some rummaging, but eventually he found a bowl and spoon before grabbing the milk from the fridge.

Not thirty seconds after Matt sat on one of the brown, high-back bar stools and took his first bite, he heard the door open and close. Oliver was home this early? Dates didn't end this early in New York.

He stopped mid-chew when Oliver stepped into the kitchen, feeling like a kid who got caught with his hand in the cookie jar. Or like he did at that party years ago when he'd gotten shit for the dessert he ate.

But then Oliver smiled. He looked so damn young when he smiled. Always had. He was the golden boy next door that you imagined on an old TV show.

"You found my stash," Oliver said as he walked into the kitchen.

"Did you try to hide them from me, or do you keep them hidden from everyone because you're embarrassed about your secret love of marshmallows in cereal?"

Oliver laughed—a rich, joyful laugh that always sounded genuine—before he walked to the cabinet and reached for one of the red bowls. He went for a spoon next and sat beside Matt at the bar and poured himself a bowl; he chose the chocolate. "If I was hiding them from you, I would have done a better job. I knew you'd go looking for them."

The same way Matt knew he would have them. Only, Matt didn't eat this as much as he used to. "The chocolate is new."

"My tastes have become more sophisticated since we were kids," Oliver teased, and this time they both laughed.

Oliver always had Lucky Charms in his house growing up. It was his favorite and so his parents made sure they always bought it. It sounded silly, but something like that was a treat for Matt as a kid. His dad was disabled and his mom uneducated. His parents had done the best they could, but it hadn't ever been easy to make ends meet. He and Oliver would sit around and eat a whole box of Lucky Charms in one day at Oliver's house, which was a luxury he didn't have anywhere else. It had taken him a while to do that, of course. In the beginning, even when they were hanging out, he hadn't wanted to eat Oliver's food at all. It had felt like a handout but of course, Oliver wouldn't have it. It was their thing—the Lucky Charms. They'd sit around laughing, eating cereal, and playing video games. They were some of the best times Matt could remember.

"Yeah, real sophisticated," Matt finally commented on what Oliver had said. "Remember when you bought me three cases for my birthday?"

"Oh my God. I was an idiot! Yes, I remember. Miles gave me so much shit for that."

Matt tried not to groan at the mention of Miles. Even though the group spent so much time together, he often felt like Miles only dealt with Matt because Oliver wanted him around. "Yes, but then we all got high and ate three boxes. Miles didn't mind then."

There was another laugh before Oliver said, "No, I guess he didn't," followed by, "I haven't gotten high in years. Not since college."

Matt took a bite of his cereal, chewed, swallowed and then looked at Oliver. "Parker and I used to get high every once in a while, just for fun. He always said I got the munchies too bad to do it often." Matt laughed. "I would have gotten too fat."

He took another bite as Oliver frowned. "What?" Matt asked.

"Not that I'm saying you should be a pothead but getting fat should be the least of your worries and the last reason you don't allow yourself to do something you enjoy. You've never had a problem with your weight. You're even skinnier than you used to be."

Matt shrugged, not wanting to get into it with Oliver. Maybe it was vain of him, but sometimes he felt like the way he looked was all he had, and he'd known Parker hadn't meant anything by it. "Remember when we got stoned, tried to make Rice Krispies treats, and we burned up that pan melting the marshmallows? I thought your mom was going to blow a gasket."

"What do you mean *we* burned the pan? That was all on you. You were in charge of melting the marshmallows."

"No, I wasn't."

"Yes, you were."

"No, I wasn't," Matt added, and they both burst into a fit of laughter. He couldn't remember the last time his gut cramped so hard from laughing, especially when he couldn't even say what was so funny.

He just knew he'd missed this. He hadn't realized how much he missed spending time with Oliver until this second. Because right now, as they ate bad food and acted like kids, everything else was gone—the career he hated and the anxiety he felt every time he had to do it. Parker, New York, all of it disappeared, and it was just Matt and Oliver again.

CHAPTER EIGHT

T HEY FINISHED THE rest of their cereal in near silence. When they were done, Oliver pushed his bowl away...not sure what to say. It was weird, not knowing what to talk to Matt about. Or at least, not feeling comfortable in the silence. When they were teenagers, it didn't matter if they were talking or not. When he was with Miles and Chance it didn't matter either, but the quiet between them right now felt heavy and awkward. What had happened to them?

"You didn't have to cut your date short because I'm here, Ollie. I feel bad," Matt told him.

Oliver huffed. He'd really fucking hoped he wouldn't have to talk about this. "It wasn't you. He has this..." Oliver almost mentioned the postnasal drip thing but decided against it. "He wanted to have a threesome. I got there, and his roommate had dinner and wine with us. He went to his room while Eddie asked me if I wanted to sleep with both of them."

"Oh shit. You've gotten fucking dirty since I left." They both chuckled, and then Matt nudged his arm. "I'm sorry. I know that's not your thing. Did you care about him?"

"No." The answer came easily. "I probably should have just fucked them and had a good time." Chance definitely would have. Miles might have; it would depend on his mood. He was pretty sure Matt would have too. Maybe Eddie was right and he *was* too uptight.

"Nah. That's not you. I always admired that about you—you're true to who you are no matter what."

Stunned, Oliver opened his mouth to reply, but nothing came out. He wasn't sure what to say. He sure as hell hadn't expected Matt to tell him he admired him. Especially after the way Oliver had practically judged Matt about his own relationship earlier.

"I'm always surprised there's not more romance in those books you write," Matt added. "You've always been ruled by your heart." Now *that* prompted Oliver to speak.

"You read my books?" He wrote thrillers, his most popular about an FBI agent named Davis. Even though his books sold well, it still gave him a thrill of shock when someone read them. Especially someone he knew.

"Of course I do. Am I not supposed to?"

"No. They're off limits for you," Oliver teased him. "I don't know why I'm surprised. Chance and Miles don't read them." Which he understood. They supported him in other ways and always bought his books. Chance just wasn't a big reader and Miles preferred non-fiction. "I know none of you like books the way I do."

"Well if Miles and Chance don't do it, then of course I wouldn't, or what?" Matt grabbed both of their bowls and went to the sink, dumping the milk. Oliver hadn't imagined the edge to his voice.

"That's not what I meant at all. I just didn't realize."

Matt leaned against the counter, crossed his arms and looked at Oliver. "Davis is a lot like you—loyal, big-hearted. Did you have fantasies about being a cop you didn't tell us about? Or you just want to bang a cop? That's why you haven't settled down. No one else will do."

Oliver rolled his eyes and stood as well. He walked to the island and rested his elbows on it, facing Matt. "No, I don't have an FBI agent fantasy, though Davis is sexy. And actually, he's getting a new partner in the next book, and you'll be happy to know Davis finally ends up getting some. No matter how hard Davis tries, he can't seem to resist the other man."

"He's gay?" Matt asked with a smile. "I just thought he was too busy or picky to want to fuck."

Another similarity between Davis and himself. "He's gay…but busy too." He ignored the picky part.

"See? You *do* have a cop fantasy. I knew it. So when we go out, I just know to get you laid we need to find someone with handcuffs. You might be even kinkier than the rest of us."

The way his friends made it sound sometimes, it was as though they thought Oliver didn't enjoy sex. Like they had to work to get him to fuck. He enjoyed sex. A lot. He wanted to fuck just as much as the rest of them. He just liked it to mean a little more than they did. It wasn't that he'd never had a one-night stand because, well, orgasms with someone else were even better than orgasms with himself. "If you find a sexy Davis for me, I just might take you up on that offer. But just so you know, I am able to get myself laid when I want to."

"I know that. Do you think I don't? You're a fucking catch. Any man would love to be with you," Matt told him, and damned if those words didn't warm up his insides. Fucking Matt and the effect he had on Oliver.

"Apparently I had two of those men chomping at the bit to-night," he teased but Matt didn't take the bait.

This felt good, just talking with Matt like this, spending time with him. Which is why he didn't want to ruin it with talking about heavy shit. Unfortunately, that was the way Oliver worked and he'd drive himself crazy if he didn't say what he wanted to say. "Have you told your parents you're here? I know they'll want to see you."

Matt dropped his head back and looked up at the ceiling. Oliver saw his Adam's apple bob when he swallowed. "What the fuck is wrong with me? I shouldn't dread seeing my own parents."

But Oliver knew he did. He didn't completely understand why, but Matt always struggled with them. He had difficulty with most people. He didn't open up too easily. He opened up more with Oliver than he used to with anyone else but still, it was always bits and pieces of whatever it was that went on inside Matt and not the full picture. "I can go with you," Oliver offered, but before the words were out of his mouth, Matt was already shaking his head.

"No. I'm not a kid anymore. You don't need to save me or protect me or take care of me." Matt's voice went harder, tougher. He pushed off the counter.

Um, what the fuck? "Hey, that's not what I meant. I'm just trying to be a good friend."

"I know." Matt sighed. "I know you are. I'm not mad I'm just…an asshole, I guess. It's my issue, not yours. I'm tired, I think I'm going to head to bed." Matt walked to him, leaned over and pressed a quick kiss to Oliver's forehead before pulling back and walking away.

Oliver's eyelids closed. "Night, babe," he said.

"Good night," Matt replied before Oliver heard his footsteps move away…and then they paused. "You kept it," Matt added softly. Somehow Oliver knew exactly what he was talking about.

"Yeah. My mom wanted to get rid of it when she had the house remodeled. I don't know why I took the damn thing. It's not as if I play it." He was pretty sure they both knew he kept the piano because of Matt. Because it reminded him of Matt and if Matt ever wanted to play it, he wanted it to be there. But then, Matt didn't need him to do things like that for him anymore, did he? If he was interested in playing, he could buy his own piano. The sad part was, he didn't even know if Matt still loved music the way he used to.

"Thank you," Matt replied quietly before walking away without waiting for Oliver to respond.

When he heard Matt on the stairs, Oliver opened his eyes and let out a heavy breath. Why was it this man got to him so much? He didn't know why he was upset, but he was. He had absolutely no reason to be, so he wiped down the counter tops, turned off the lights, and headed upstairs. He took a quick shower before climbing under the beige comforter on his plush bed. Not a second later, his phone beeped. He knew exactly who it would be.

"Leave me alone, Miles," he said instead of hello.

"You're home, aren't you? I knew you'd be home!"

"So? You're home too." At least he assumed Miles was.

Miles ignored his question. "Did you go out?"

"I did. I swear. Eddie thought it was a good idea for him and me to fuck his roommate, despite the fact that I haven't even fucked him yet. Not my scene."

"Ouch," Miles replied. "Then I guess you're excused. You know I only care about you, Oliver. I don't want you to get hurt, and I don't think Matt would ever hurt you on purpose. He's not malicious but…"

"He doesn't feel the same," Oliver cut him off. "And I know you only care about me. That's why I put up with you, but it's been a long time. Just because I'm different from you and Chance doesn't mean I'm the same kid I was. I'm not wearing my heart on my sleeve when it comes to Matt. Hell, I'm not even still tangled up in him the way I was. It's just…he's my friend and I missed him. It's good to have him back, that's all. I know what I'm doing."

There was a short pause. Oliver clutched the phone and waited. "Okay. You're right. Plus, I think I hit my emotional quota for a while anyway. I'll go back to being a surly bastard now."

"You're a softy; you just can't admit it."

"Fuck you! Bite your tongue, Oliver Hayes. I'm hanging up on you now."

He laughed when Miles did just that. Oliver set his phone on the bedside table, rolled over and tried to go to sleep.

CHAPTER NINE

MATT'S PARENTS WENT to church every Sunday morning. When he was younger, the only time they missed a week was if one of them was able to pick up an extra shift at work. His mom always said God was more important than money, but God also wouldn't have given them the chance to support their family a little better on a Sunday morning if he hadn't meant for them to take it.

Despite the fact that Matt gave them money, they still lived in the same small, two-bedroom house he'd grown up in. They'd been able to fix it up a bit but, *"What did they know about living anywhere different?"*

That had been his dad's bit of wisdom. The difference now was they could afford to get something new when they needed it. They didn't have to take the bus…and his mom didn't have to pick up extra shifts on Sunday or any other day for that matter. She still worked because that was how she rolled, but she could work her regular hours just like everyone else. And she also didn't have to work two jobs anymore, which meant she wasn't employed by Oliver's parents any longer.

Matt sat in a rental car in front of the old, white cement house, knowing his parents would be back any minute. He'd gotten up early this morning, not surprised to see Oliver was already awake as well. The man had always been an early riser. Now he woke up early to write, he'd told Matt, but he hadn't gone into his office this morning. He'd taken Matt downtown so he could rent a car, so he could sit in it and be fucking weak as he dreaded going inside again.

Jesus, he felt like such a bastard sometimes. He wanted to believe most people were just like him, only they didn't admit their selfishness quite as easily as he did, but hell, that just might be him trying to make himself feel better.

Loud music played in the background, getting closer and closer before a tricked-out car drove past, with bass so hard Matt's windows rattled. As the car pulled by, he saw a silver Toyota heading in his direction. He knew the car. He'd helped his parents get it nearly two years before—which honestly, had been like pulling fucking teeth. It hadn't been brand new, his parents insisted on that, and even then it had taken a whole hell of a lot of work for him to get them to take it.

Matt understood that, though. It was that exact reason he'd left LA. He didn't want to depend on someone else. He wanted to succeed on his own.

He watched as the car slowly pulled into the driveway. Watched as his mom got out of the driver's seat. She was a short woman— skinny with brown hair that matched Matt's, which she always kept in a bun. He got the shape of his lean body from her.

She opened the passenger door for his dad, who was a burly man. He stood a good foot taller than his mom. Matt was closer to his dad's height, but that was where the similarities ended between them. He had a beard, as he always did. Blond hair, dark eyes, and even now when he pushed himself out of the car using a cane, his chest and arms were hard to miss. Maybe it was all the years of hard work or just that he'd been born with burly DNA, but he definitely hadn't passed it on to Matt.

There was a deep ache in his chest as he watched his dad hobble on the cane. He was too young to need it, but years of manual labor and injuries he never reported and worked through had come back to haunt him.

He'd been devastated when he had to stop working. Felt like they'd stolen his manhood, he'd told Matt. Men were supposed to work hard, were supposed to support their family. It was the only time in his life he remembered thinking his dad might cry.

He hadn't, of course. Rusty Daniels didn't cry, but it had been close. Matt used to feel guilty when he'd cry as a child. Not because his father would harass him for it but because he could see the confusion that was always in his dark eyes. See the detachment, the wall that was between them because his dad just couldn't understand why Matt was so different from him. He didn't doubt there was disappointment too.

"Fuck," he gritted beneath his breath. Why the hell did he do this to himself? He was who he was, and his dad was who he was, and neither of them could change it.

Before he did something stupid like drive away, Matt opened the door and stepped out. Just as his parents made it to the porch, he called out, "Mom! Dad!"

His mom whipped around in his direction. His dad's movements were a little slower as he held onto the railing and turned. His mom's hand went to her mouth and Matt knew it was shaking. Knew she was crying because he hadn't seen them in years.

Not knowing what else to do, he shrugged and stepped around the car. "Surprise."

That was when his mom came running for him. She leaped into Matt's arms. He made an *umpf* sound but caught her as she hugged him and cried into his neck.

Guilt and regret made a lethal cocktail inside of him as he held his mom and stared at his dad who stood on the porch watching them.

"You're here. I can't believe you're here," she said softly against his skin as his dad smiled at him.

He let her down and she turned toward the house. "Rusty, Matt is here!" She opened her arms and hugged him again.

"I think he can see that, Ma. Can you see me, Dad?" he called, trying to keep the mood light.

"Where is he, Jolene? I can't see him!" he called back and his mom pulled away and swatted Matt's arm.

"That's enough, you two."

"Hey." He rubbed where she hit, pretending it hurt. "Why'd you hit me? He said it."

"You started it. Why didn't you tell us you were coming?" She grabbed his hand and began dragging him toward the house. Matt hit the lock button on the key fob just as they made it to his dad.

"It was a last-minute thing. I just decided I needed a short trip so I figured it would be a nice surprise."

"Nice? It's the best surprise." She gave his arm one more squeeze.

He and his dad looked at one another awkwardly, as though neither of them knew what to do. The truth was, they didn't. It was his dad who made the first move, giving Matt a small nod before he said, "It's good to see you, son."

They wouldn't hug. That wasn't how they were so Matt just returned the nod and replied with, "It's good to see you too."

His mom reached toward his dad to help him but then pulled back as though she thought better of it. He didn't like to show any weakness. Matt knew the cane was bad enough for him. He wouldn't want to accept help in front of anyone, so he used the railing and his cane to hobble up the three steps.

"We should get you guys a ramp," Matt said without thinking.

"I don't need a ramp. It's fine."

"I've been telling him that for months. It would make things much easier," his mom said as she unlocked the barred screen door before unlocking the main door next.

"I'm fine," his dad gritted out for the second time. It was on the tip of Matt's tongue to say that he wasn't, that it was okay to have help but he didn't want to fight with him.

They made their way into the kitchen. His father sat in one of the chairs as his mom asked if he wanted anything to eat or drink. "No thanks. The place looks good." He let his eyes roam the kitchen. The wallpaper was gone with a fresh coat of paint now applied.

"Because of *you*. I don't know how we'll ever repay you." She sat at the table. It was a dark, almost cherry wood, small and square with four chairs around it.

"You don't have to repay me. You guys supported me for eighteen years. It's the least I can do." They'd worked their ass off for him. They'd tried to indulge his desire for music and arts, even when it set them back. Even when the things he wanted were like a foreign language to them. Things they couldn't understand their son wanting.

"That's what parents are supposed to do. That's not what their children should have to do." She looked down and he knew she felt guilty for not being able to give Matt the things she felt he'd deserved. Growing up, he felt similar guilt for wanting things that were so different from what his family had. For wanting things like Oliver, Miles, and Chance had. For feeling so fucking out of place in his own skin and his own home.

"Anyway," she shook her head, "is that what you're in town for? Work? I still can't believe it. Can't believe what my boy has accomplished."

Remorse spread through him like a Southern California brush fire. How sad was it that he gave them no reason to feel like he would come home for anything other than work? Work that he didn't want, work that he'd begun turning down. Work that every time he did it—made his pulse race and his vision swim and his hands shake.

He was so fucking blessed. The two people at the table with him now had worked themselves into the ground, but Matt had been refusing jobs for months, for what? Because he hated it? He didn't doubt his parents had hated the work they'd done. Because it made him want to jump out of his own skin? His dad had ignored worse, actual injuries for years.

"No, not work. I just…felt like getting away." He couldn't even use his breakup as an excuse because he'd never talked to his family about Parker. It was almost as though his life in New York and his life in Los Angeles couldn't coexist. It wasn't like he hid his sexuality. They'd known he was gay since he was fourteen. He'd never wanted or been able to hide that fact, but they didn't talk about who he dated. Parker never came home with him and they didn't exchange Christmas cards or anything like that. "I missed you guys," he added because it was true. Despite the edginess he often felt in their presence, he missed them.

"We missed you, too." His mom reached out and cupped his face. "But you look too skinny. You tell them you'll be just as beautiful with another ten or fifteen pounds on you."

On reflex, Matt's eyes darted toward this father. The other man cleared his throat, looking anywhere except at his son. Matt didn't turn away and waited for what he knew would happen. There was no surprise when his father worked his way to his feet. "I'm tired. I think I need to lie down for a little while. It's…it's good to have you home, Matt," he said, and even though he didn't know how long Matt would be there, he hobbled out of the room.

This was nothing new, though. They'd never known how to talk to each other, and they likely never would.

CHAPTER TEN

E VER SINCE OLIVER got home from taking Matt to get the car, he'd done nothing except stare at a blank computer page. He left off with Davis and his new partner, Tony, arguing about how next to try and find their serial killer. Of course, they argued about everything because the men were as different as night and day.

He rarely struggled to figure out what to write next. It had always come automatically for him, even going back to his script-writing days, but somehow he wasn't surprised that today he wanted to throw his computer out the window. Or just write Davis boning some guy—Tony or someone else because writing sex felt like the easiest thing to do, especially since he wasn't having it.

"Fuck," Oliver whispered as he dropped his head back against the chair…then spun the seat around like he was five years old. He was totally going to blame this on Matt. He'd shaken up Oliver's routine and now he was all out of whack. He was thinking about their conversation last night and what things would be like when Matt came home. How long he would be here and Matt, Matt, Matt, Matt, Matt.

Oliver glanced at the time in the upper right-hand corner of his laptop. It was one o'clock. Matt would have likely been with his parents for close to two hours by now. His mom would fly; she'd be so happy to see him. Jolene's face always glowed when she saw or talked about Matt. He didn't think his friend saw it, though. Didn't think he realized how proud she was of him.

No, things hadn't always been easy on them, but he had no doubts how the elder Daniels felt about their son.

Rusty would be awkward…quiet. He'd always been stoic—keeping to himself no matter what had happened in their lives. It always bothered Matt because he didn't see what Oliver did…that in more ways than he realized, Matt was a lot like his father. The way they kept their emotions close and didn't let people in. The way they didn't want to lean on anyone.…Matt had gotten that from his dad.

And thinking about Matt and his family was not going to help Davis and Tony solve their dilemma. Damn Matt for fucking with his thoughts again.

Oliver flicked a pencil across his desk and then grabbed his phone. He needed to get out of here—to clear his head and there was one place he usually went to do that.

He had just taken a step out of his office when the front door opened. He heard Matt curse quietly, then a moment after, call out, "Hey, Ollie. I'm back."

He smiled and rolled his eyes. When they were teenagers they got to where Matt spent nearly every day at his house. Eventually, Oliver told him to just come in—that it was a hassle to come to the door when it was only Matt.

Of course, Matt had nixed that idea. It was too vulnerable for him, but then one day he'd gotten so used to being there that he'd just walked in. It hadn't been until he walked into the living room and Oliver looked up at him from the couch that Matt had realized it. The wide-eyed look on his face had told Oliver that.

Oliver shrugged and told him, "It's okay, Matty. This is a second home to you."

He'd been able to see the embarrassment there. The color in Matt's cheeks. But he'd rolled his eyes and said, "Your lazy ass just doesn't want to get up to answer the door."

"And your bossy ass just wants to make me do it." But even back then, he'd known that wasn't it. That Matt hadn't felt comfortable until it happened without his intent.

And now, years later, he did the same thing the second day he was back in LA.

"Oliver?" Matt called, and Oliver stepped out of the darkened hallway where he'd been pathetically thinking about the past.

"Hey." *How'd it go?* He wanted to know but he didn't ask.

"Hey. You working?"

He should be. "No. My muse isn't cooperating. He needs some stimulation."

"So you're jerking off then?"

Why did Matt's reply not surprise him? "Already tried that."

"Must be serious if an orgasm didn't help. Especially after your failed threesome attempt." Matt winked.

"Fucker," Oliver replied, shaking his head but Matt didn't keep their teasing going.

He cocked a dark brow at him and crossed his arms. He wore a tight-fitting, light pink T-shirt with a V-neck and a pair of jeans Oliver knew likely cost more than any of the clothes he'd ever had as a kid. "I guess The Getty will have to do then," Matt continued.

Without any direction from his brain, Oliver frowned. It shouldn't be, but it was a little unsettling how well Matt knew him sometimes. How he knew what Oliver needed without much thought. "How did you know?"

Matt almost looked hurt at the question as he cocked his head and eyed Oliver. There was something in the set of what was usually a delicate jawline. He finally answered with, "Come on. How could I not know?"

And that was the thing—no matter what, Matt knew him. He'd known Oliver for years, honestly, in ways even Chance and Miles didn't know him. He wasn't sure how that had happened since he'd known Chance and Miles longer, but it was the truth.

The museum always relaxed him. It always helped him clear his head. Made him feel at ease in his skin. He'd minored in art history and always had a love of art, and Matt remembered Oliver's private routine of going to the museum. Of course he did. "You're right, dumb question. Davis is fucking with my head."

"Probably because it's three books in and he hasn't gotten laid yet. You should write more sex."

Matt reached back and opened the door. "Can I go?" he asked. Oliver didn't reply, merely looked at Matt until he said, "You're right, dumb question,"—the words Oliver had just said to him— and the two of them walked out of the house to spend a day together the way they'd done too many times to count.

THE FIRST TIME Matt had gone to The Getty was with Oliver. He hadn't understood it then—Oliver's desire to go to the museum because he'd had a bad day. How the fuck could that help?

They were about…fifteen years old. Oliver had been stressing himself out because they had to do a method acting piece for their drama class and he didn't think he could do it. He'd always put a lot of pressure on himself with anything he did but he hadn't needed to. He always succeeded in whatever he tried.

"You'll be fine," Matt had told him because he knew it was true. There wasn't anything Oliver couldn't do, but he'd nearly had a panic attack, and Matt suggested they do something to get his mind off of it. He sure as shit hadn't expected Oliver to say The Getty but he had, so Matt had gone, and somehow…it had helped.

He'd gone often with Oliver over the years. Chance and Miles only went one time with them. Other than that, it was always just Matt and Oliver. That was why he couldn't understand the reason he'd acted surprised Matt had mentioned it. Had that much space really wedged between them? Did he really think that Matt could actually forget important parts of who his best friend was? The thought made him sad. He was determined to fix it, to bridge the gap he'd created because Matt knew it had been himself, not Oliver who'd done it.

"It's been a long time since I've been here," Matt said as Oliver drove up North Sepulveda Boulevard.

Oliver glanced his way. "Ten years. We never went when you came back to visit, right?"

No…no they hadn't. Matt suddenly wondered why that was. Sure, he hadn't been out in a few years, but in the beginning, he'd come yearly. Why hadn't he suggested doing something he knew Oliver loved so much? "No, we never did. So the last time would have been a few days before high school graduation."

"And fucking Chance almost got us kicked out."

He'd been typical Chance—loud and boisterous but even more so because they were so close to graduating. Oliver had nearly lost his mind while Matt was stuck between thinking Chance went too far but also chuckling at Oliver's reaction. They were polar opposites in some ways, those two. Oliver serious and Chance carefree. "I thought your head was going to explode. You nearly lost your fucking mind."

"He pretended to hump a sculpture, Matty."

Matt could see it clear as day now—Chance making it look like he was taking the statue from behind. A laugh burst out of his mouth at the memory. God, they were fun. Despite the awkwardness that was sometimes there, he had a lot of fun with Chance and Miles too. "He was so fucking crazy. Is he still that crazy?"

Oliver glanced his way again. "Is that really a question? He's Chance. Yes, he is. I haven't been back here with him since and likely never will."

Matt laughed again, not surprised Oliver had held a grudge

about it. Oliver took that shit seriously. "I'm sorry. Now I feel even worse that we haven't gone together in so long. I'll make it up to you. I'll be sure to try and come out at least once a year and when I do, we'll hit The Getty together."

Oliver turned into the parking lot. Matt could see his forehead crease even from the side view. "I appreciate that. Miles likes to go with me, though. It's something we do fairly often together, and I'm a big boy now. I don't mind going alone." He glanced at Matt and winked, but Matt felt a strange twist in his gut. What did he expect? Oliver would never go to The Getty with another person because he left? It was unfair for him to feel almost…jealous about it, about the thought of him and Miles doing something together that had always belonged to Matt and Oliver. But he'd left, hadn't he? And he didn't visit for years.

"You're frowning," Oliver said.

"No, I'm not," Matt told him. "Why would I be frowning?" But he was and he knew it. He was being a selfish bastard, expecting Oliver to hold onto something that had belonged to them when the reason they couldn't do it together anymore was on Matt.

"Miles doesn't have a problem with you. He never has. I know he comes off as a dick, but he's the same way with you as he is with everyone else."

And that was part of it, wasn't it? He likely wouldn't have been as hurt if Oliver went with Chance. Matt never believed Miles thought he was good enough to be friends with Oliver.

"Fuck." Matt ran a hand over his face. He was too old to have this conversation anymore. Too old to be jealous of Miles. He'd made something of his life on his own. He'd grown up, changed. Miles could like him or not like him and Matt would be just fine.

Oliver pulled into a parking spot before Matt continued, "I'm not the same kid I was. I don't need Miles's approval. I don't need anyone's approval. I know who I am now in ways I didn't back then." He was Matt Daniels. He lived in New York City. He was a model. He'd clawed and fought his way to where he was, and he wasn't going to let it slip away, no matter how at odds he felt with himself right now. No matter how much of it felt like a lie. It couldn't be. If it was, who the fuck was he?

He saw the questions in Oliver's big, round eyes. He was doe-eyed, always had been, questioning and searching everything.

"You didn't need anyone's approval, even back then. Maybe that's not the way you see it. Maybe you thought you did, but you didn't. You've always been strong enough to do your own thing; sometimes it just takes you a while to realize it."

Oliver's words slammed into his chest. Tried to take his breath but Matt fought against it. He knew they were talking about music. Oliver romanticized everything. It was easy to do when you'd always had what you wanted. He didn't mean that as an insult to Oliver because he'd never acted the least bit spoiled. It wasn't who he was, but there had also never been anything Oliver couldn't have. He saw the world through the rose-colored lenses because that had always been his life.

But that wasn't Matt's universe. Yeah, he was fucking lucky to have what he did and to be where he was but he knew there weren't a hundred other options waiting for him. It was why he had to keep going, why he had to get his fucking head back in the game because this was his life. He'd worked too damn hard to get a hair up his ass, feel sorry for himself and risk losing it. "And sometimes I realize when something isn't meant to be. Not everything is, Ollie."

Oliver paused, worked his jaw but then he nodded. "Yeah...yeah, I guess you're right."

And they weren't only talking about music.

"Come on." Matt nodded toward the window. "Let's go. I think I need to be here with you today."

Oliver didn't respond. He only returned the nod and got out of the car.

CHAPTER ELEVEN

*A*ND SOMETIMES *I realize when something isn't meant to be. Not everything is.*

That little bit of truth Oliver had always struggled with. No matter how much he wanted to believe otherwise, not everything he wanted was meant to be. It was idealized thinking to believe it was.

Miles and Matt both saw the world that way—they were more similar than either of them realized—but Oliver never had. He wanted to believe anything was possible. That he and Matt were meant to be. Matt would compose and his group of friends would always be happy and close and life would never get in the way....But life did, didn't it? More than Oliver wanted to admit.

He heard Matt suck in a breath beside him. "I forgot how beautiful it is up here." He loved the architecture. The beautiful white building on the hill. The view of Los Angeles below.

And it was. That was why Oliver loved it so much. They made their way inside the building and into a large open area. It was stark white, except for the color in the paintings on the wall and that of the people walking through.

"You should come visit me in New York sometime. I'll take you to The Met."

That was the first time Matt had ever asked him to New York. Matt had been gone ten years and he'd never visited him there. Before, he would have jumped at the suggestion but now he shrugged and said, "Yeah, maybe."

They made their way through the quiet room. There was nothing but abstracts here, which Oliver had to admit weren't really his thing.

They were mostly quiet as they made their way from room to room. Matt let Oliver lead him, following behind him as he took in all the art. He'd always been creative, always known he'd wanted to do something in the arts. For a while, he'd thought acting until he settled in with his love of words. It made more sense anyway. Oliver was more comfortable in his books than anywhere else, which was why it frustrated him so badly when he struggled.

"Ollie, look at this," Matt said in a hushed tone.

He hadn't realized Matt had snuck away from him. He was in an archway that led toward another section of the museum. Oliver followed him over. He hadn't taken the time to look online to see the current exhibits. He never did. He enjoyed not knowing what to expect when he came. It made the experience more exciting and interesting.

The first thing Oliver saw when he walked into the room was a photograph of a man. He was naked, sitting backward on a chair, facing away from the camera. His arms were over the back, his body slouched as if he leaned over it, with his head down. His body language screamed sorrow, melancholy, but that wasn't what caught Oliver's attention. No, it was the artwork on his back. He had a huge piece—a dragon tattooed onto his skin. It almost looked as sad as the man. As painful.

"Tony needs a tattoo," he whispered.

"Who?" Matt asked.

"Tony. He's Davis's new partner. He lost his family when he was a child. It's why he became an investigator. He needs a piece on his back that represents his loss." It didn't hit him until right now. No, this knowledge didn't solve his current issue with Davis and Tony but it was another building block in Tony's character. It helped him connect with Tony more, which would make it easier for everything else to fall into place. Oliver and Davis were different in so many ways but in others, he knew Davis so well, he felt like an extension of himself. That wasn't the case with Tony.

"It amazes me you can do that." Matt's arm brushed against his; they stood so close. "My mind doesn't work that way. I couldn't just have something click into place the way you do. I remember that from high school when you used to write all those stories. We could be anywhere and you'd pull your phone out and type in an idea because of a random man you saw in the parking lot or a display in a store window."

"Please." Oliver nudged him with his elbow. "It's not as if you don't do incredible things. You started playing the piano, by ear, with no lessons for years. You used to compose music like it was as easy as breathing. It's a part of you. You can try to deny it all you want, not mention it at all but it's still a part of you." He was likely overstepping his bounds. This wasn't his place but Oliver couldn't let this moment go without having said what he did.

Matt sighed. "Are we back here already? Sometimes I think you forget that the fantasy worlds you create aren't real life."

He wanted to know what had happened to Matt to make him believe he couldn't pursue his dream. What had happened to the determined man who'd left here ten years before…or was Matt right and was Oliver living with his head in the clouds? Matt had accomplished great things. Not many people could go on to do the things he had. Dreams changed. Maybe music really wasn't Matt's dream anymore.

And Oliver needed to stop trying to help Matt when he didn't need it. Stop trying to give him things that Oliver wanted him to want because then he still felt like the boy Oliver used to know. "Jesus, I suck. Maybe you'd like me to cut your sandwich into four squares at dinner too?"

Matt chuckled and then reached out and grabbed Oliver's hand. He let him, feeling the warmth in his smaller fingers and palm.

"It's just because you care. I get that and…I missed you, Ollie. You've always been the best friend I've ever had."

Matt was the best friend he'd ever had too.

THEY FINISHED THE exhibit of contemplative and emotive photography before making their way to the next floor.

Oliver spent most of his time taking in the pieces, all the art that he loved so much—and Matt spent his time watching Oliver. He wondered what kind of clarity Oliver received when he was here. If he was getting the answers he sought as he sat on a bench or eyed a piece of artwork.

They'd been here a few hours before Matt noticed the time. Since it was Sunday, the museum closed at five thirty, which wasn't too far away. "You know we have to make it out there, right?" Matt couldn't come to The Getty with Oliver and not go out to the gardens. They'd never skipped them before and he didn't plan on doing it now.

"We do. I was waiting for you to mention it," Oliver replied before they began to head that way. There were numerous gardens there, but it was the Central Garden that Matt and Oliver had always spent the most time at—with its tree-lined paths, ravine, and scents of nature.

It was quiet once they immersed themselves in the trees and began making their way through the garden. Oliver had his hands shoved into his pockets—Matt's arms were crossed. He dropped them to his sides, realizing how stiffly he stood. It was only a few short moments later that the words snuck out unplanned. "He's getting worse."

Oliver sighed, obviously knowing who Matt was talking about.

"I know…but he's okay. He's strong. Maybe the surgery will help if he goes through with it."

Matt's heart banged against his ribcage. "What? Surgery?" He didn't know anything about a surgery.

He could see the regret in the wrinkles around Oliver's eyes when he looked at him. "Fuck. I'm sorry. I didn't know they hadn't told you. I only heard it from my mom. Apparently, he's not sure if he wants to go through another surgery on his back, even though this one would be different."

But they hadn't told him. Why the fuck hadn't they told Matt?

"It's likely because they didn't want you to worry until they decided if they were going to go through with it or not."

Logically, Matt knew that made sense…but they'd spoken to Oliver's family about it. But then…other than today, when was the last time Matt had a conversation with his mom that lasted longer than ten or fifteen minutes? When was the last time he'd dug deep during those conversations? When had he really asked how things were going with his dad?

No, he couldn't only blame them. Matt was upset, that didn't change, but it wasn't only their fault.…*I started trying to pretend my life here didn't exist.* The truth knocked the air out of him, and he stopped moving, dropped his head back and looked at the sky. "Everything feels so fucked up, Ollie, and I can't say why."

He sighed, walked over to the beige bridge which led over the ravine and leaned against it. "I felt so awkward at my own house today—with my own family." Yes, he always had in some ways, but the divide between them seemed to continue to grow. "And the second Mom mentioned my career, Dad got flustered and left the room. He looks at me and it's as though I'm from another universe. He doesn't want to see me that way. I know it, but somehow that makes it worse." If his father was just an asshole—a bigoted prick or something like that—it would make things different, but the fact that his dad wanted to try and understand Matt but couldn't, made him feel like an intruder in his own family.

The railing on the bridge creaked when Oliver leaned against it, as well. "Why don't you come home more often?"

"I don't know." And the award for being the biggest liar of the day belonged to Matt.

"Liar," Oliver replied, calling him out on it and then, "are you happy? Modeling and living in New York…are you happy?"

He thought for a moment. He'd had a lot of good times out there. He'd grown as a person, had experiences he wouldn't have had in LA. Even Parker, they'd had too many good times to count, but did that mean he was happy? The answer should have come easily. He should be happy but the truth was, he didn't know how to be. No matter what he did, he wasn't happy so he answered with, "I'm trying to be." And he was. He wanted to feel joy in his life. Who didn't?

Oliver sighed, wrapped an arm around Matt's shoulders and pulled him closer. There was a warmth to Oliver that only he had. Like he somehow had the power to put people at ease just by being him. It's why everyone liked him so much. It's why Matt hadn't been able to keep himself from letting Oliver in.

"Then start now. Have fun while you're here. Figure out what's going on in that crazy fucking head of yours, and then go back to New York and do what you've always done."

"What's that?" Matt asked.

"Fight. Dream. Want."

Matt tried to turn away but Oliver grabbed his face. "You've always been a fighter. You learned the piano when you couldn't afford lessons. You succeeded, made people believe in you and showed them you were a fucking force to be reckoned with. Where did that Matt go?"

Matt wanted that. Wanted to fight so fucking bad because he

wanted Oliver to be right about him. He wanted to be the kind of man Oliver respected and spoke about the way Oliver was speaking about him now. In some ways, Ollie was right. Matt hadn't been the guy to take no for an answer before. He played when all the odds were against him, and he didn't know how he'd lost that part of himself. But he wanted him back.

And damned if he didn't want to be happy too.

CHAPTER TWELVE

T HEY GOT BACK to the car and Matt surprised him when he
said, "I don't feel like going home yet."

"Are you hungry?" Oliver's mind was running. Davis and Tony
were rambling in the back of his head and he couldn't make them
shut up. Not that he wanted to. Hell, he needed them to open up
to him. This whole relationship thing was uncharted territory for
Davis, who had always been a workaholic.

But then his stomach also felt like it wanted to eat itself, so he
thought maybe putting some food into it was a good idea.

"That works. Can we go somewhere on Sunset?"

"At your service," Oliver teased, causing Matt to chuckle before
he began to make his way back down the hill. Every so often, he'd
glance Matt's way—see him look out the window as they drove
through Los Angeles. It was loud and there was traffic and horns
blaring. As crazy as it sounded, it comforted Oliver in a way. There
was nothing more familiar to him than the city he'd lived in all his
life.

"I miss it sometimes. The vibe here is completely different from
New York. It took some getting used to in the beginning."

"Did it?" Oliver asked, stopping at a red light. There were a few
homeless people on the streets, teenagers walking, a full bus stop.
He wondered how it felt to look at Los Angeles from the outside
and imagined Matt feeling that way in New York. "You never said
anything."

"That's because I was a stubborn eighteen-year-old kid who didn't want to admit I'd gotten in over my head."

The light changed and they began to move again, albeit slowly. "The stubbornness hasn't changed."

"Fuck off."

"Defensive, are we?" This moment felt like it had when they ate the Lucky Charms last night. Jesus, had it only been a night? But Matt looked relaxed...comfortable, as though no time had passed between them. Maybe he really was going to let go and enjoy his time here before he went back to his life in New York City.

"You know me, right?" Matt asked, making them both laugh.

But then, Oliver, who never knew when to stop, asked, "What happened when you first moved to New York? The guy and stuff."

Matt groaned. "Are you going to make me do this?"

"I'd like it if you would."

He put his elbow next to the window. "What do you think? He was a guy I met online. He wanted a live-in, young fuck buddy. I was there three days before he made that obvious and when I didn't want to suck his dick, I was out."

Oliver's hands tightened on the steering wheel and his heart damn near stopped. "I fucking knew that was dangerous! Why didn't you say anything? Jesus, Matty, he could have fucking hurt you! I would have sent you money and you know it."

"Jesus, Ollie," he returned Oliver's words. "I wouldn't have wanted your money and *you* know it. I was fine. I figured it out. It was ten years ago. He didn't hurt me and I survived."

But he shouldn't have had to survive that. He should have had support....But he hadn't wanted Oliver's support.

When he remembered hearing the man ask for a blowjob as they'd spoken on the phone years ago, he wondered how many men wanted sex from Matt. How many men looked at him and just saw how fucking gorgeous he was and wanted a piece of his ass.

"We were having a good time. I don't want to talk about this," Matt said.

It took everything in him not to force the issue, but Matt was right. It had been ten years ago, and Matt was fine.

It wasn't until Oliver heard the soft song playing in the background through the speakers that he stopped, a goofy-happy smile pulling on his lips.

"Oh shit!" Matt said before Oliver had the chance. He reached over and hit the button to turn the volume up to hear the beginning of "My Humps" by The Black-Eyed Peas.

It was Matt who started singing with Fergie first. Oliver tried to hold back his laughter but couldn't as Matt went on and on about his *lady lumps,* dancing and using hand motions at the same time.

When it came to the second verse of the song, he looked Oliver's way with so much joy and passion in his eyes that Oliver couldn't stop himself from opening his mouth and taking over. They obviously hadn't done this in years, but it came right back to him. Funny how lyrics to a song that held memories for you never went away.

They danced and sang at the top of their lungs as Oliver drove down Sunset Boulevard—taking turns with which one of them took the lead. Matt didn't stop smiling the whole time, didn't stop dancing and trying to look fierce as hell.

Oliver felt fucking ridiculous—like he was a teenager being fucking silly and crazy in the car with his friend, but he didn't care. This had been their jam back then, and nothing would take this moment from them.

When the last few beats of the song finished, the two men dissolved into laughter again. Oliver's heart thudded against his chest as he gripped the steering wheel. Matt's laugh was electric—contagious in its joy as he struggled to catch his breath. He'd forgotten what it sounded like to hear Matt let loose, to have him live in the moment. It was a beautiful thing.

"Oh shit. I needed that," Matt said when he finally settled down. He dropped back against the seat with a hand on his stomach as though it hurt from laughing so hard.

"My cheeks feel tingly from laughing," Oliver told him.

It took Matt a minute to respond and Oliver was surprised when he answered with, "We've always had so much fun together, haven't we?"

Yeah…yeah, they had. Oliver didn't answer right away, though. He slowed down when he saw a parking garage. The restaurant was a block or two up but they likely wouldn't get parking closer than this.

He turned inside and when the car went dark, he said, "Of course we have."

"Promise me we'll never lose this. I know it's my fault. I stopped coming home and cut people off, but promise me we won't lose it, Ollie."

He fought to keep himself from closing his eyes. From letting his emotions take over and asking Matt why—why he'd stopped coming home and why he'd cut Oliver out.…Why he seemed so lost right now…but instead, he only replied with the truth, "Of course we won't lose it." Because Matt would always mean something to him, even though he knew they would only ever be friends.

⌇

THEY WERE SITTING on the patio of a little Italian restaurant as people walked down Sunset. Matt loved to people-watch. He always had. It made him really feel like he was home to sit out here with Oliver and observe all types of different people walk by.

The conversation hadn't stopped at all. They didn't discuss anything important, and he was glad for it. Not because he didn't want to share—scratch that, in all honesty, he didn't want to talk about himself—but because discussing those things made him remember that he'd come here because he felt disconnected with his life. Right now, he just wanted to ignore those things, shove them in the back of his mind and pretend they didn't exist.

"Can I get you guys anything else?" the waiter asked after stepping up to their table. He was a young man—probably twenty or twenty-one, with red hair and freckles that were fucking adorable.

"I think I'm okay. What about you?" Matt asked Oliver.

"Are you sure? You didn't eat much," Oliver replied. Matt shook him off. His eyes darted up as he made eye contact with the waiter, who blushed.

"I'm okay. Thank you," Oliver told the waiter who nodded and then looked at Matt again.

Oh, fuck. He knew what was coming next.

The kid spoke with a lowered voice when he said, "I'm not supposed to do this but I have to.…You're Matt Daniels, aren't you?"

"Um…yeah. I am." His stomach immediately twisted into knots that he fought damn hard to shove away. He hated this kind of attention on him, but he smiled his flirtatious smile that projected the opposite.

"I knew it!" the boy said a little too loudly. He looked around before speaking with a hushed tone again. "You're even more beautiful in person. I'm an aspiring model. I've done a few small shoots…nothing that really makes any money or anything but…I went to Hollywood Academy of the Arts too. I was able to get in on a scholarship because…well, you don't need to know my life story but I just wanted to let you know I really admire you. *Oh my God*, I can't believe I'm meeting you right now."

Matt immediately felt like invisible walls were closing in on him. He couldn't see them, but he felt them squeezing the space around him so it was smaller and smaller.

He wasn't really anyone to admire. Here this kid was—whose dream it was to model, and Matt only did it because he didn't have a choice. Because it was easier to get by off his looks. Not that modeling wasn't hard work. It was and he respected the hell out of everyone that did it but for him, he didn't burn for it the way this kid did. He didn't have the fire in his eyes the way he did.

Every time he was in front of the camera, he wanted to hide, to close in on himself.

He couldn't say that, though.

"Hey, thank you. I appreciate that. It's nice to meet you." Matt held out his hand. His eyes darted to the boy's nametag. "Bailey."

"Thank you. It's nice to meet you too."

They shook hands and spoke for a minute before Bailey told him, "I need to get back to work, so I don't get into trouble. Thanks for being so gracious. Not everyone is."

Matt shrugged. "Thank you for introducing yourself. I'm not sure I deserve the admiration, but I'm incredibly thankful for it." And he was. How could he be thankful for something but resent it at the same time? "You keep doing what you're doing and you'll make it. One day I'll be able to say, I met Bailey at lunch and he was incredibly gracious and down-to-earth."

The boy's eyes blazed brighter. "Thank you. Holy shit, I can't believe this. Thank you so much. I'll be back with your check." And then Bailey disappeared. The second he was inside, Oliver spoke.

"You should be proud of yourself, babe. You worked hard and you made it but you haven't lost who you are. You made that kid's day because it was the right thing to do, while part of you wanted to crawl out of your skin because you're uncomfortable with the attention." He wasn't surprised that Oliver noticed how he felt. Maybe that was part of the reason he'd stayed away. Oliver would see the things he could lie to everyone else about. He also wasn't surprised his friend called him out on it.

"I don't know if *crawl out of my skin* is the best way to put it." But maybe it was. He could tell Oliver how his nerves were getting the best of him, how having eyes on him was getting more and more uncomfortable. That it was hard to make it through photo shoots sometimes. That there were moments he thought he would lose his mind, but he didn't. He couldn't. The truth was, he just had to deal with it.

"In some ways you've changed, and in others you haven't changed at all." Oliver cocked a brow at him and Matt was pretty sure that wasn't a compliment. Before he could respond, Bailey came back with their bill. He pulled his card out before Oliver had the chance.

"I got dinner," Matt told him. He turned to look at Bailey. "This is my friend Oliver. If it wasn't for him, I wouldn't have been able to go to Hollywood Academy of Arts. His family sponsored me. I never expected to make anything of my life, but I did. You work hard and you can make your dreams come true too, Bailey."

"Oh wow. I didn't know that. Thank you," Bailey told him again. When Matt risked a glance at Oliver, he saw the question there before he forced himself to look away. *Did your dreams really come true, Matt?*

Oliver opened his mouth to respond but was cut off by the sound of Matt's phone. Bailey took his card and left as Matt considered ignoring Parker's call. He couldn't, though. He needed to talk to his agent.

"I have to get this," Matt told him before he answered with a "Hello?"

"Hey, I take it everything is good?" Parker asked.

There was no real emotion in Parker's question. Matt didn't fault Parker for it. He knew his ex-boyfriend and current agent cared about him; that just wasn't how they'd ever really worked.

"Yep. Good to go. I feel more relaxed already." It was actually true.

"Good. I have a proposition for you. I'll email you the information, but I know how you are with that shit. It'll take you a month to respond to it. There's a job coming up in LA. They want you for it. It's a simple spread for a magazine, but it's in two weeks. I'm not sure how long you planned to stay, but I thought that might work out for you. You'll be rested and recuperated. You won't have to hurry home."

"Are you trying to get rid of me?" Matt teased him, even though the truth was they had a lot to work out. At least, he did. He lived in Parker's apartment. They had to figure out what would go on with work. Or that was another thing Matt had to make a decision about, at least.

"No. You know that. There's always room here for you. I'm just…we need to figure out what you're doing. Is this a permanent vacation? Are you done working? Just slowing down on the job?"

This didn't surprise him. Parker was fierce when it came to his work, as he should be. But still, "It's only been a couple of days since I left."

"Say no if you're not ready. I just thought I'd offer. They want you but if you can't do it, you can't do it. I just thought it made sense considering you're already there."

Matt glanced at Oliver as though he would have the answers for him. As soon as he did, Matt forced his eyes to dart away. He didn't need Oliver or anyone else to make his decisions for him. "Send me everything I need to know. I'll check it out and get back to you tonight but yeah…unless there's a big reason for me not to do it, I will."

"That's my boy," Parker told him. "Have fun with lover man." Parker hung up the phone. Yeah, they definitely should have broken up long ago. They were better off as friends. That much was obvious.

"Everything okay?" Oliver asked. His voice was filled with concern that was typical of Oliver.

"Yeah, it was Parker. He has a shoot for me to do in LA in two weeks. You okay with being stuck with me that long? If you want your house back—"

"You just want me to ask you to stay with me." Oliver winked at him.

It was the only answer Matt needed.

"Now that we have that settled, let's go. I'm taking you to Sprinkles for dessert."

Matt pushed to his feet and tried to ignore the weight that suddenly sat in his gut. Two weeks. He'd be ready to get in front of the camera again in two weeks. It was time he got over it.

CHAPTER THIRTEEN

THERE WAS SOMETHING going on with Matt when it came to his work, but Oliver couldn't put his finger on what it was. He'd looked nervous as hell when Bailey spoke to him at the restaurant the other night. He'd become tense and rigid when he spoke to Parker on the phone about the upcoming job. He wasn't happy. It didn't take a genius to figure that out, but there was more to it than that.

He also knew there was no way in hell Matt would just come out and tell him. It had been in the back of Oliver's mind as they'd gone about their week, which had actually passed by smoothly.

Oliver wrote like hell every day, the words forming in his brain faster than he could type them out. Their trip to the Getty had been exactly what he needed....Or hell, maybe it was because things had felt normal between him and Matt since then.

They'd had cereal for dinner twice—Matt complaining that Oliver was going to make him get fat and cause him to lose his job. They'd laughed and watched movies and spent their evenings together. It was good to have Matt back. It was good to spend time with his friend again.

Speaking of Matt, Oliver made his way to the open door of the guest room. "Jesus, does it always take you this long to get ready? You're worse than Chance."

Matt popped his head out of the en suite. "I'm not taking a long time. Am I taking a long time?" Oliver cocked a brow at Matt before the man added, "Fuck you."

Oliver let a soft laugh escape. He walked over to the bathroom and leaned against the door. Matt stood in front of the mirror in a small pair of black underwear that hugged his small, tight ass. His legs were long and thin. He wore a tight, baby-blue shirt that made his green eyes look a shade closer to blue.

He ran his hands through his hair, styling it by ruffling it and making it look messy. He was such a fucking contradiction. He knew Matt felt uncomfortable with too much attention on him but in a way, he called for it. He'd always flirted and looked to hook up and made himself look good in ways Oliver himself had never given a shit about. It wasn't because Matt was conceited. People thought that of him, but Oliver had never been blinded enough to miss the self-doubt hiding behind Matt's beauty.

"You're looking at me funny. Why are you looking at me funny?" Matt's brows knitted together.

Oh shit. He had been. Goddamned wandering mind and eyes when it came to Matt. "Because you're funny-looking, pretty boy. Now get some fucking pants on before Miles and Chance show up here looking for us."

"People usually want me to take my pants off, not put them on." Matt winked at him and Oliver rolled his eyes. He should have seen that one coming.

"Not me. Your butt is too small for my taste." *Total fucking lie.* Matt's ass would fit nicely in his hands. Who didn't love a small, tight butt?

"Really?" Matt looked over his shoulder as if he'd never seen his own ass before. "It's proportionate to my body. If it was much bigger I'd look lopsided." He turned back and eyed Oliver again. "And I have to tell you, I've never had complaints before. I've made many a strong man scream with this ass. It should be considered a dangerous weapon."

Oh Jesus Christ, he was ridiculous. "I'm going to strangle you and then my hands will be the only dangerous weapon. Get your damned pants on before I leave you behind." Oliver pushed off the counter and walked out of the bathroom before he bent Matt over and showed him a dangerous weapon of his own, that most definitely wasn't his hands.

Matt sighed before Oliver heard him click the light switch. By the time Oliver made it to the door Matt said, "It's going to feel weird seeing Miles and Chance again."

Yeah...yeah, Oliver figured it would be. Still, he turned and asked, "Why?" as Matt grabbed black pants that lay on the bed and began pulling them on.

"You know why, Ollie. Come on. Don't pretend you don't."

Matt was right. He shouldn't have. "They're your friends. They missed you too. I don't know why the awkwardness is there between you and Miles, but it'll be fine. I promise."

"Oh, fuck. Now I feel like an asshole. You just sounded like you were talking to an eight-year-old. *It'll be fine, baby. I promise. Daddy will take care of you.*"

"Can you please never call me that again?" Oliver teased, making them both laugh.

"Fucker," Matt said before pulling out a pair of socks and slipping them on. He pushed his feet into a pair of black shoes next. "How do I look?" he asked.

Matt really didn't want Oliver to answer that honestly. Oliver didn't want to answer it honestly, either. What he wanted was to go out with his friends and have fun. To enjoy Matt while he was here, not to want him so damn much and to feel okay about it when Matt left for New York.

So he lied and instead of telling Matt he was a wet dream, he shrugged and said, "You'll do. Now, let's go."

WILD SIDE.

The sidewalk outside of the bar Oliver went to every Friday night was packed with people. This, of course, wasn't anything new in West Hollywood. Matt remembered being a kid and talking about when they would be able to hit some of the bars here together. He felt a little twist in his chest that Oliver, Miles, and Chance had been doing that together for years without him. He had no right to feel it because he could have been here with them—even if it was just when he came to visit—but as much as people liked to pretend they did, emotions didn't often make much sense.

They got out of the car and the Uber driver sped away as Matt heard the faint competing beats of music from neighboring bars. He would be lying if he didn't admit that his pulse kicked up a notch. Maybe he didn't play anymore, and yeah, the style of music was different from what he'd written and played himself, but any kind of music felt like its own heart in his chest. Like he had one to keep him alive and one for music.

"Come on." Oliver locked a finger with his and led Matt over to the line. As they went, he noticed a couple of men gaze toward Oliver. Watched eyes roam his body, which made Matt do the same. Oliver was an inch or two taller than he was, broader.

He wore crisp, dark blue jeans and a red Polo shirt that showed off his arms.…Arms that looked bigger, more toned than they had in high school. *Huh.*

"What?" Oliver turned to him, making him realize he'd said it out loud. Oliver's short, blondish hair looked as though his hands had raked through it a few times. He had these hypnotic, chocolate eyes—wide and innocent. He understood why men looked at him. It wasn't that he'd never thought Oliver was an attractive man because he always had. But when he looked at his friend, he'd always seen Oliver's kindness first. His compassion. Seen how he held himself back sometimes and let the world move around him if that was what he thought was better for others. He saw the things that Oliver had done with him, the help he'd given and the laughs they'd shared but fought to allow admitting the things he noticed now.

But he got it, got why men were looking at him and wondered why Oliver didn't take advantage of that more often—but then that was Oliver, wasn't it? Nothing was only skin deep with him. He wanted things to mean more. He ran off his heart more than anything else.

Again, he wondered why Oliver wasn't in a committed relationship. Wondered how someone hadn't seen how fucking incredible he was and snatched him up. There had to be a man out there for him, someone who deserved him.

"Do I have food in my teeth or something? Now you're the one looking at me funny," Oliver said, pulling him out of the thoughts he'd often tried not to have. They moved up in line a bit.

"You grew up good, Ollie," Matt admitted honestly.

There was a brief flash of shock in Oliver's face before he steeled it. "Well obviously not that well if you're just noticing." He laughed it off but Matt didn't join him. Oliver always brushed off compliments, but he never stopped giving them to others. It was just the way he was built.

"I'm serious. You're gorgeous and you look good. If you weren't my best friend, I would definitely try to get in your pants tonight."

"Oh stop." Oliver waved him off playfully, but Matt noticed the faint blush on his face. Noticed the way his pupils grew and those doe eyes of his opened more.

"You've been eye-fucked by like three men just since we've been in line."

"They were probably looking at you," Oliver said as they moved a few more feet up in line.

A wave of unease slid down Matt's spine but he ignored it. This was about Ollie. "Fuck off. I know what I saw. They were looking at *you*. We should get you laid tonight. You owe yourself after how everything went with your date the other night."

Oliver's whole body visibly went tense, and Matt wondered if he'd gone too far. If maybe he was stepping over his bounds, but fuck that. Oliver always spoke up when he thought it could benefit Matt, so why couldn't Matt do the same for him? "Come on." He put his hand over Oliver's heart and tapped it twice with his fingers. "I know you run off this, and that's so fucking rare and beautiful in this world, but it's okay to enjoy yourself too."

Oliver stepped back, making Matt's hand fall. "You sound like Miles—except without all the heart talk if it was coming from him. Believe me, I know how to fuck when I want to. It was just under a week ago you got here and I was going out, remember?"

The discomfort from the moment before settled at the base of his spine. He didn't know why. Of course, Oliver went out and got laid when he was horny.

"You're shocked. Jesus, you're actually fucking surprised. Why the hell do all my friends think it's their responsibility to help me get laid?"

"I volunteer!" the man in front of them said and laughed.

They ignored him. Shame made Matt's bones feel too heavy— like they didn't fit in his body anymore. "Fuck. You're right. I'm sorry. I don't know why I said anything."

He could still see the frustration in the set of Oliver's body. In the wrinkle above his brows.

"Because you think it," Oliver replied.

Or maybe it was easier to concentrate on Oliver than all the shit going on with himself. Or just as likely, he wanted to give some- thing to Oliver, wanted Oliver to need something from him, even if it was only advice and a compliment because Matt had always needed something from Oliver. "You're probably the last person who would need help with anything. I don't think it's my responsibility to get you laid. It was a dumb thing to say, and I'm sorry. I say stupid things around pretty boys, and there are a whole hell of a lot of them here, counting you." Matt cocked a brow at him. "Ignore what I said and have some fun with me tonight. I've been looking forward to hitting up WeHo with you since I was a kid." The line moved again, putting them at the front. Matt latched his hand with Oliver's again, stepped in front of them and paid the cover before pulling them both into Wild Side.

CHAPTER FOURTEEN

MATT TRIED TO lead Oliver toward the left, where the bar was, but Oliver tugged his hand. He didn't know what that had been about in line, where all that shit had come from with Matt, but he didn't like Matt to see him that way. It was one thing for Miles and Chance to give him hell about getting laid, but it cut a little deeper with Matt. He didn't want Matt to think he sat around, never going out or going home with men because he was too damn emotional for anything else.

"Over here," Oliver finally told him. "We have a table in the corner that we always use."

Matt nodded at him. This would be the first time Matt saw Miles and Chance in years. Chance would be fine. Chance was okay with everything, but he'd be lying if he didn't admit a small twitch of nerves under his skin when it came to thinking about the interaction between Miles and Matt.

They worked to make their way through all the dancing men and women. When their table came into view, he saw Miles and Chance already sitting. Dare, the owner of Wild Side and his boyfriend, Austin, stood beside them.

"You're late," Miles said when they approached.

"Shut up, Miles," Chance said as Matt replied, "It was my fault."

Chance stood first. His skin glistened slightly with sweat, telling Oliver he'd been dancing even though he didn't work tonight. He wore a T-shirt cut off so that it showed his lean stomach and a pair of form-fitting jeans.

"Hey, Matty. It's good to see you," Chance told him as Oliver let go of Matt's hand and watched the two men hug. He caught Miles's eye over the two of them and Miles rolled his before he stood as well.

"You look good," Matt told Chance when they pulled away. Chance winked at him.

"I know."

"And you haven't changed, either," Matt replied, chuckling. He turned to Miles next. "Hey, man. Long time no see."

"Yeah, it's been a while since you've been out. Glad you were able to make time," Miles replied, and Oliver had no doubt that Matt heard the subtle dig in there.

"There won't be that much time in between visits again," Matt replied to him before they gave each other a brief hug.

Wanting to derail any opportunity for drama before it started, Oliver said, "Matt, this is Dare. He owns the bar, and this is his boyfriend, Austin. Austin works at the LGBT Center. He runs a great teen program over there. Dare and Austin, this is Matt."

A crease formed between Dare's brows. "You look familiar…"

Oliver inwardly groaned. He didn't think Matt would want to go there tonight. Hell, he wasn't sure Matt ever wanted to go there.

"Just one of those faces, I guess." Matt smiled. "Great bar you have here."

That got Dare off the subject of Matt's face. They spoke for a few moments about Wild Side, the LGBT Center and surfing. Dare was a long-time surfer and Austin had started getting into it with him since the two men had stepped out of the friend zone and into a relationship.

Dare and Austin weren't able to stick around for very long. Dare promised to send drinks over and Austin was going to head to

Dare's office to read. He'd recently told Oliver he'd read his books, which Oliver appreciated but was still something he struggled to get used to. It was awkward sometimes to have people he knew read his books. What if they hated them? He also didn't want anyone to ever feel obligated just because they knew him.

"Miles told me about Postnasal Drip!" Chance said to him when the four of them were seated at the table alone.

"Postnasal drip?" Matt asked.

"The dude Ollie was dating. We were discussing the pros and cons of getting head from the guy because apparently, he had mucus issues. He solved the problem for Oliver when he tried for the threesome. We all know our boy doesn't go there."

"Hey!" Oliver nudged him. "I could have a threesome if I wanted to," he replied.

"You didn't tell me about the snot," Matt added, a smile pulling at his lips.

"There's a reason for that," Oliver told Matt and then looked at Chance. "And seriously, I could have a threesome. I just didn't fucking know that guy from Adam and Eddie sprung him on me."

"I want to have a threesome with a guy named Adam…or Eddie," Chance said and Oliver wanted to smack him. "Oh, minus the phlegm, though."

Everyone at the table erupted into laughter except for Oliver.

"Gee thanks, Matty. I thought you would be on my side. Can someone explain to me why every time we get together we end up discussing my sex life?"

"Or lack thereof." Miles winked at him and even though he wanted to kick him under the table, there was a part of Oliver that was glad Miles involved himself in the conversation, even if it was at his expense.

"Tell me about this guy," Matt said to Miles. "Apparently, Ollie didn't give me any of the good stuff."

Miles started talking to Matt, who laughed at Miles's exaggerations. There was a moment where Oliver wanted to tell all of them to fuck off but when he glanced at Chance and his friend gave him a small grin, he knew that Chance had done this on purpose. He'd found a way to break the ice between Matt and Miles, most likely because he knew that was what Oliver wanted.

And it was great. The conversation didn't stay on Eddie for long. They talked about bad hookups and fucked up Grindr messages. Work and play and family. They laughed and it was just like old times. For Oliver, it was perfect.

MATT WAS DRUNK as hell.

They all were. They'd downed drink after drink as the four of them lounged in the booth Oliver, Miles, and Chance sat at weekly and talked.

He couldn't remember when he'd had so much fun. It was sad, really. Not the fact that he had fun with his oldest friends, Miles included, despite the tension that was often between them. No, it made sense that he had a good time with this group of men. But on the other hand, it was sad that he never just had fun like this anymore. That any time he and Parker had gone out lately, Matt had felt alone, no matter how many people they'd surrounded themselves with.

He hadn't realized just how long he'd been pulling away like muscle from bone in a sporting injury.

He'd been pulling away from life, and damn it—he was starting to get emotional drunk.

"Let's dance again," he told Chance before he let himself get into a funk.

He'd always had a good time with Chance. How could he have forgotten how much fun they had together?

For the third or fourth time that evening, Matt and Chance made their way to the dance floor.

Chance was a beautiful dancer. Matt could just sit back and watch him sometimes. When they were younger, they spent a lot of time watching him dance.

But as Chance grinded against him and Matt closed his eyes, it became more than about dancing or Chance. It was about the music. He breathed it in, smelled it in the air, studied the sound in his ear.

He fell in love with it the way he'd done hundreds, if not thousands, of times in his life.

It didn't matter what genre of music it was when it came to listening—every sound, every beat, every note made his heart pulse because those sounds were someone's love the same way his music was his.

With each moment that passed, the joy he'd been feeling began to fade. Sadness grew and expanded in his chest. He missed this. Why wasn't he doing this? *Because you couldn't....Because you failed.*

And then as if Oliver could sense his pain, he was there, his arms around Matt and dancing with him. Matt wrapped his arms around Ollie and held him tight, let the music wash through him as Oliver surrounded him.

"You ready to go home, Matty?" Oliver whispered in his ear.

"Yeah." He really shouldn't have drunk so much.

The two men said their good-byes to Chance and Miles. Before he knew it, they were in an Uber, then the car was pulling up in front of Oliver's house and they were walking inside.

"You okay?" Oliver asked as he closed the door.

"Yeah, I'm good." And he was. He was just drunk.

"You never have been able to handle your alcohol well."

"Exactly! So you're not supposed to let me drink that much!" Matt teased, trying to bring himself back from the edge.

"I'll keep that in mind next time." Oliver grinned at him and Matt's heart sped up. Jesus, he was really fucking drunk. They were standing close, so close, and Matt noticed a small scar by Oliver's mouth that he'd somehow never seen before.

"I should go up…to bed…"

Oliver didn't reply. He just kept looking at Matt and Matt wondered what it was he saw. What he'd always seen in Matt that made him reach out, that made Oliver care about him the way Matt knew he did.

The way that meant so fucking much to Matt, even though he'd never let himself voice it.

And then Oliver's arms were around him. He hugged Matt. His lips pressed softly to Matt's forehead before he leaned down and pressed his own forehead against Matt's.

"Tonight was fun," he said softly. "It was good…spending time with you, Chance, and Miles like that. I missed it. I missed us."

He knew Oliver meant "us" as in talking about the four of them but in that moment, it was only the two of them. Oliver, his friend he cared about so much but who he'd held himself back from for so long.

They started moving closer. When Matt's lips moved, they brushed against Oliver's. He did it again…and again. He felt Oliver's breath when he whispered, "Matty…"

Matt went to reply; what he was going to say, he didn't know. Oliver didn't give him the chance, though. Before Matt knew it, Oliver was pulling away. "I'm pretty tired myself. I think I'm going to head up. I'll see you in the morning."

Matt watched Oliver until he got to the top of the stairs. Damned if he hadn't wanted to call out to him, to go to him and do what? Another thing he didn't know, which was why he let Ollie go. It was better that way.

He couldn't let himself go upstairs right now. If he did, he was scared of what he would do, so Matt made his way into Oliver's living room. He ignored the piano in the corner, went toward the built-in bookshelves by the window.

They were full, stuffed with book after book after book. Some of them Oliver's and some of them not.

He wasn't sure what drew his eyes to the book with the white spine and the author he didn't recognize. Actually, that was a lie. It was the word *Music* in the title.

Matt pulled the book off the shelf, walked over to the couch, and started to read.

CHAPTER FIFTEEN

OLIVER HAD NEVER been a very heavy sleeper, so when the soft melody of the piano drifted up the stairs, he heard it. He glanced at the clock on his bedside table. It was six a.m. He had no idea what had happened between midnight and now—between their foreheads pressed together and Matt's lips brushing against his—but he was playing. Matt was fucking playing for the first time since he'd been back and Oliver wanted nothing more than to go downstairs and watch him. Oliver needed to see him, to feel Matt's music up close. He'd always loved watching Matt play. It was the only time in his life that Matt fully opened up. The only place he felt comfortable, Oliver guessed.

But even as his pulse seemed to match Matt's music, he didn't let himself go downstairs. Didn't want to take this moment away from Matt because he'd found it. Somehow, he'd found it. Oliver closed his eyes for a second and let himself breathe it in. This was the Matt he knew, the one with his fingers roaming up and down black and white keys. He didn't know if this was *still* who Matt was, if his passion had dimmed and turned into his past or if there was another reason he kept himself away from the piano he used to love.

Not my business, Oliver told himself before forcing his eyes open and climbing out of bed. He made his way to his en suite and closed the door, muffling Matt to the point where he only heard a note here or there. He put his hands flat on the counter and leaned close to the mirror. He smelled Matt's cologne, the scent of alcohol on his breath, and remembered the feel of Matt's nose brushing against his.

"Fucking Oliver. Stop this shit," he said to himself before he walked over to his shower, pulled the glass doors open and turned the water on. He was only wearing a pair of boxer-briefs so he stepped out of them, kicked them to the side, and stepped into the shower.

He tipped his head under the hot spray, trying to wake himself up, trying to keep himself from going down to listen to Matt play.

Music was different from writing, obviously but he thought about how it would feel to have someone sit in the room with him if he'd just sat at his computer for the first time in God knew when. It would feel like stealing something from him, taking a piece of the thing he loved from him, and he wouldn't let himself do that to Matt.

Oliver tried to push him out of his head as he showered. He let the water try to wake his muscles and bones up, before he soaped himself, washed his hair, and got out.

He pulled the black, plush towel from the rack, rubbed it across his hair before drying off and wrapping it around his waist.

And then he was still.

Pretty fucking pathetic too, as he listened for Matt playing and heard nothing. It hadn't been very long—maybe half an hour tops since the gentle music had first woken him.

Oliver opened the door and took one step into the room before his eyes hit Matt. Matt sitting on the side of his bed wearing nothing but a pair of black shorts. His dark brown hair looked wet as it hung against his forehead, a veil between Matt's eyes and him. Had he showered before he'd gone down to play? Tried to talk himself out of it the same way Oliver had forced himself not to go downstairs?

Matt's right leg bounced up and down like a jackhammer as he looked at the floor and didn't speak. Oliver didn't either. He didn't know what to say, so he just took another step into the room, and then another.

It was then when Matt's head tilted up, that he shook his hair off his forehead and his eyes met Oliver's searing with something that he didn't understand. He thought maybe there was some pain in there…a little confusion but more that Oliver couldn't read.

His breath caught when Matt pushed to his feet. The shorts hung low on his slender hips, and he was sure Matt didn't have underwear beneath them.

His chest was smooth. He had a light trail of brown hair that dipped below his shorts, which hung so low he could see the top of Matt's pubes.

Despite how thin he was, too thin if you asked Oliver, his muscles were well defined. He had a lean six-pack that rose slightly as Matt breathed.

Jesus, he was so fucking sexy, so beautiful it seemed unreal.

Matt moved toward him again. His gaze turned more predatory as chaos erupted inside of Oliver—pain and confusion and lust…was that what he saw in Matt too? Lust was the missing piece?

His thoughts went haywire, snapping and buzzing with years of pent up energy. And then he was moving toward Matt too. He didn't know what they were doing, didn't know where it came from—at least on Matt's part—but the second they met in the middle of the room, their mouths crashed together. Matt's hand slid behind his head, cupped it with his fingers, tangled in Oliver's wet hair. Oliver's fingers locked onto Matt's lean hips, felt his hipbone press into his hand and he wanted to get on his knees and taste them. Wanted to lick and suck and explore every fucking inch of Matt's body with his tongue.

"What are we doing?" he asked when Matt's skillful mouth traveled down his throat.

Matt sucked on the spot where his neck met his shoulder, before he replied, "I don't know, Ollie. I just know…know that I need you right now."

He could hear Matt warring with himself, hear it in the rough edge to his voice. Feel it in the way his body tensed up when he said the word *need*. It wasn't easy for Matt to need anyone or anything, but Oliver would take on the fucking universe to make sure Matt had it. There wasn't a time in his life when he wouldn't but this moment right here? He couldn't pretend this was just for Matt. Couldn't pretend he wasn't greedy for him, that the fire searing through him for Matt was based on anything more than his primal hunger for the man. To have him, take him, fuck him, even if it was only once. He'd wanted Matt for years, loved him since he was a kid—and as they stood in the middle of his room, Matt's hand running up and down his back, his cock pressed against Oliver's leg, he damn sure planned to have him. In that moment, he didn't give a shit about the consequences.

Oliver wrapped his arms around Matt, lifted him up, their mouths still fused together. Matt's legs wrapped around his waist, knocking Oliver's towel free as he carried Matt to the bed.

He bent over, lay Matt down and went right along with him, nestled between Matt's legs, with his feet still on the floor.

He pulled away long enough to say, "Jesus, you taste so fucking good," and then he was kissing Matt again, letting his tongue roam Matt's mouth as he thrust his aching prick against him.

His brain tried to tell him it was a mistake, that he shouldn't be doing this but Oliver ignored it. Right now he didn't want to be logical. He didn't want to worry about consequences or his stupid fucking heart. In that moment, he just wanted sex, wanted to have Matt, so he ignored his brain and kissed his way down Matt's neck, his chest, his stomach, until he kneeled on the floor between Matt's legs, his hard rod evident behind his shorts.

He palmed Matt's cock through his shorts, felt the heat of it despite the material. Matt hissed, moved his hips so that his shaft pushed into Oliver's hand harder.

"Take me out.…Please, Ollie. Take me out."

"Ask me again," Oliver told him as he continued to work Matt through his clothes.

"You're gonna make me beg for it?" Matt asked. Oliver wouldn't; they both knew that. There wasn't a doubt in his mind that Matt knew better, but still, he opened his mouth and said, "Take out my cock, Oliver. Let me feel you. I need to feel you."

Oliver's fingers shook as bursts of electricity shot through his body. He grabbed the top of Matt's shorts and pulled them down his thighs as his prick sprung free. He was long, thinner than Oliver himself, with trimmed pubes and a heavy sac. Across his left hip was a tribal tattoo that would typically be covered by his underwear. He leaned forward and kissed it. Let his tongue trace the swirls and lines. Lust pummeled him, made Oliver even more ravenous for him as he pulled back and situated Matt's legs on one side of him so he could pull the shorts all the way off.

He leaned forward, inhaled Matt's scent—soap and musk. He fucking swore he felt something rumble inside of him, a hunger he couldn't control. This was Matt. *Matt.* Oliver would get to be inside him, fuck him, feel all that heat as he took him, and afterward, maybe Matt would do the same to him.

Oliver tongued Matt's sac with one long lick, lifting his balls and watching them fall. He did it again, and again, lapping at his sac as Matt's hand knotted in his hair. As he pulled Oliver closer to him, nearly suffocating himself between Matt's legs.

He liked that he was making Matt so fucking wild, so fucking needy.

This wouldn't last long; he knew it wouldn't last long. Already his balls wanted to release just with the promise of feeling Matt from the inside.

"I don't think I have much foreplay in me," Oliver said before tonguing Matt's balls again. He hated the words. He wanted to make this last all fucking day—take Matt to the edge over and over before he finally let him teeter off it, but he already felt jacked up on too much adrenaline. Like he could bust his load just from playing with Matt's nuts.

"I didn't ask for foreplay," Matt replied as Oliver licked a path from the root of his erection to the tip. He swirled his tongue around the head, taking in more of Matt's heady scent and tasting his pre-come.

Oliver pushed to his feet before covering Matt's body with his own. He still lay with his legs over the edge of the bed. Oliver kissed him as he thrust his prick against Matt's. He felt so fucking good, his skin hot with desire.

Matt kissed him deeper, pumped his hips to meet Oliver's. Their balls touched. Oliver's damn near exploded.

"Fuck me. Get your goddamned cock inside me," Matt gritted out.

"Oh, fuck." Oliver stilled. His dick liked the sound of Matt's command a little too much. Oliver pulled off him before he embarrassed himself, then leaned over to open the bedside table drawer. He pulled out a condom and lube—that was really fucking close to being empty after quite a bit of solo hand action lately.

He ripped open the condom wrapper and covered himself. He grabbed Matt's slender hips and pulled him closer to the edge of the bed so that his ass hung off the side, really thankful that he had a high bed.

Matt stroked his pretty cock, spread his legs and that was when Oliver got the first glimpse of his hole—tight, puckered, and pink. Jesus, there was nothing he wanted more than to be inside of it, to breach him, take Matt deep until they were like puzzle pieces snapped together. Long strokes, short strokes, fast, slow. He wanted to do it all, bury himself in Matt and stay there until he couldn't fucking take it anymore.

The knowledge hit him then, that it wouldn't be enough. He'd been lying to himself and that made him feel really fucking weak. It was sex. He should be able to fuck without attachment. People did it all the time. He'd done it before, but this was Matt and everything was different when it came to Matty.

"Oliver?" Matt said and the mood in the room immediately changed, became heavy. "Christ, I shouldn't have asked you to do this. I thought…I wanted…hell, I don't know what I thought or what I wanted."

He tried to get up but Oliver put a hand on his chest and didn't let him. "It's just sex," he said, the words burning his tongue. "It was inevitable we did this once, I think." His voice didn't sound like his own, but he wanted those words to be true. He would fuck Matt, he wanted to fuck Matt, they'd both come and the novelty would have worn off. "I just…Jesus, that's a sexy fucking hole, Matt. I got distracted by your ass. You can't blame me for that."

"See?" Matt smiled. "I told you I haven't had any complaints about it before. I'll drive you fucking wild. You wait and see."

A tremble rocked through him. He had no doubt about what Matt just said.

Oliver opened the bottle of lube, squirted some in his hand, and ran it up and down his aching erection. He squirted more onto his fingers, rubbed it against Matt's tight pucker and pushed inside. His knees nearly gave out, it was so damn hot inside him.

He leaned over him, pushed Matt's legs back, lined his cock up to Matt's ass and then pushed his way inside. It took him a few seconds to work his way in, to stretch Matt's hole for his dick. When Oliver was finally buried to the hilt, they both shuddered.

"It's all right," Oliver forced himself to say.

"Did you just say my ass is only all right?"

He felt Matt clench and he damn near blew his load. "It's fucking incredible."

Oliver pulled almost all the way out and then thrust forward again. He took Matt with long, hard strokes. Their bodies slapped against each other. Sweat slicked their skin. He felt Matt's hipbone each time he slammed into him. He wanted to put a little weight on him. Not that Matt wasn't fucking gorgeous the way he was, but he felt the need to fatten him up.

Matt moved against him. Reached around and grabbed Oliver's ass as they fucked. His breathed hard in Oliver's ear as Oliver moved faster, deeper, harder.

"Oh, fuck. Right there. Christ, you're hitting my prostate just right."

Oliver pistoned into him, locked their lips together. Felt his balls draw up tight. Their lips parted and as soon as they did he heard a soft, "Oliver...Oliver...Oliver..." from Matt's lips, as his asshole squeezed tighter, spasmed, while a ribbon of come shot from Matt's dick, between their bodies. It mixed with the sweat, made them stick together each time Oliver thrust against him.

That was all it took for him to let loose, for his orgasm to shoot through him as Oliver's body went rigid....But he still kept going, kept fucking as he shot, filling the condom.

And then he collapsed on top of Matt, his body bigger than his. Matt breathed hard in his ear. His hands ran up and down Oliver's back before they stilled, and all Oliver wondered was if Matt regretted it. If he lay here under Oliver and wished he'd never come into the room.

CHAPTER SIXTEEN

"I'LL BE RIGHT back," Oliver said as he pulled out of him, turned and walked to the bathroom. Matt watched him go, watched as he took off the condom and tossed it into the trash before looking at himself in the mirror.

What was he thinking? Matt wondered. Hell, he could ask that of himself. Why in the world had he come upstairs and told Oliver he needed him? Why had he felt like he had? He couldn't even blame it on the alcohol as it had long left his system.

"Do you need a towel or anything?" Oliver asked.

Matt's voice cracked when he said, "No." He sat up, grabbed the towel from the floor and wiped the come off his stomach.

Christ, he'd just fucked Oliver. His best friend. The man who looked at him like he walked around kicking puppies when he'd discovered Matt had an open relationship with Parker. The man who wasn't into sex for the sake of sex or hooking up.

Fear suddenly clawed at him, ripped through his insides like a wild animal viciously attacking him. What if he'd screwed up? What the hell would he do if he'd fucked up his friendship with Oliver because he'd been feeling lost? Because he'd been feeling alone? Because he read a book that tore up his insides and then played the piano which shredded them more?

"We're okay, aren't we?"

Oliver headed back his way. He stood naked in front of Matt. His dick was soft now, hanging between his legs. Matt eyed his hairy thighs, the definition in his abdominal muscles and the softness in his face. He really was a gorgeous man, outside as well as inside.

"Why wouldn't we be okay? It was sex, Matt. I'm a big boy. Don't treat me with kid gloves because you don't think I can handle fucking my best friend and then moving on. We were horny. We had sex. Nothing changed. You wouldn't have asked that question if I were Chance or Miles."

"Maybe because the answer wouldn't have held the same weight." It likely made him a dickhead that he felt that way. It wasn't as if the men weren't important to him—they were. But they also weren't Oliver. Oliver would always be more important. No matter what he'd done in the past or the distance Matt kept between them, Oliver would always be one of the most important people in his world.

Oliver sucked in a deep breath and moved closer until he was standing between Matt's legs. He knew something heavy would come out of Oliver's mouth and Matt really didn't want to deal with heavy at the moment so he said, "And you're right, you are a big boy. If you don't put your cock away, I'm going to be distracted."

Oliver put his hand under Matt's chin and tilted his head up so Matt looked at him. "Hmm. That's a nice change. Maybe I'll let myself enjoy it." And then he brushed his thumb across Matt's cheek, making a tremor vibrate through him before Oliver dropped his hand.

"Look at you, being all sexy and shit," Matt told him.

Oliver sat beside him. "I try." He took a deep breath and continued, "It was fun as hell. Now I can say the size of your ass is definitely perfect the way it is."

Oliver's words almost sounded light but there was something stilted to them as well. Like they were said just to say them. They didn't have any meat to them.

Still, Matt replied with the same teasing content. "Right back at ya. Christ, you can work that dick."

They both laughed but it ended too soon. Oliver wouldn't let this go. He faced things head on so Matt wasn't surprised when he asked, "Why now?"

"I don't know," he answered. And really, he didn't but...there was more to what happened and his coming into this room too. "I read it."

"Read what?" His voice rose, slightly higher in confusion.

"Your musician, and don't try and tell me you didn't write the book. I read it, and I heard it, Ollie. Those were your words and you were writing about me." He saw too much of himself in Samuel for there to be any other answer. Music had been Samuel's heart and then he lost it, the same way Matt had.

Oliver had written a book under a pen name for him, a book about him, about finding his music and damned if that hadn't done all sorts of things to his insides. His brain, his heart, his dick. Everything.

He looked over at Oliver when there was no reply. Oliver stared back, their faces twelve inches away from each other. "No one else would have known that was me...that I wrote that book."

Matt shrugged. He wasn't so sure about that. Or maybe Oliver was right and it was something that only Matt would recognize because they'd always been in tune like that. And that book, Samuel's story...

"I don't wanna lose it permanently, Ollie...but I don't know how to find it either." There was no one else in the world he would admit that to. Not Parker. Not his family. Sometimes not even himself.

Oliver wrapped an arm around Matt's shoulders and pulled him close. His lips pressed against Matt's forehead and stayed there—*one beat, two beats, three beats* before they pulled away. "I know, babe," he said and kissed Matt's forehead again.

He couldn't say what made him do it, but Matt tilted his head up, nudged Oliver until their lips met. As Matt's mouth opened and his tongue begged for entrance to Oliver's he wondered what the hell he was doing. Why he was kissing his friend again because before it had been about sex. He knew that when he saw Oliver, but this was different. Yet questioning it wasn't enough to make him stop.

Oliver opened for him, giving him a taste. His hand went into Matt's hair and he groaned into Matt's mouth. He liked the sexy little sounds Oliver made. They urged him to grab onto Oliver's side and give him a slight tug. Oliver came easily, climbing on top of Matt as he went down onto his back.

He cupped Oliver's ass, ran a finger down his crack, rubbed his asshole but then just settled for wrapping his arms around him, letting Oliver anchor him. Christ, he hated even using the word *anchor* but from the moment they'd become friends, that was what Oliver had done for him. Even when Matt fought against it. Even when he told himself he didn't need it. Even when Matt ran away from it. Oliver's friendship was his constant.

When Oliver nuzzled his neck, kissing him there, Matt said, "I don't know if it's a good idea to make a habit out of this."

"You're the one who kissed me first."

"No, you kissed my forehead."

Oliver laughed against his skin. "And you slipped me the tongue. We sound like we're sixteen." He pressed one more quick kiss to Matt's lips before he stood. His dick was hard, tall and thick against his stomach. He had a nice cock, the head purple and swollen, with pulsing veins in his shaft that Matt suddenly wanted to taste.

Christ, he wanted to devour his friend all of a sudden. He need-ed to get that shit under control. He'd always been good at forcing himself into one box and Oliver into another. He had to, otherwise, this would have happened a long time ago, and someone would have gotten hurt.

He really fucking hoped that didn't happen now.

Oliver turned to walk away and Matt started, "Where—"

"I'll be right back." Oliver cut him off and went to his walk-in closet and disappeared inside. Matt heard a box open, heard papers rub against cardboard before Oliver came out with a thick folder in his hand that Matt would recognize anywhere. It was manila colored. The front would be full of doodles and random shit he'd drawn when he was younger. The inside was stuffed full of music that Matt had written himself—most weren't finished. They were half-done or less, all pieces he'd started but realized they were shit until one day, toward the end of senior year in high school he'd thrown them away. "How...?" He started but couldn't make himself finish.

"How doesn't matter. You didn't lose it, Matty. Even if you never use it in the way you'd hoped, even if it's never what you do, it's still a part of you. It's still there. Fuck, it's *inside* of you, swimming in the marrow of your bones. Pumping through your heart. In each breath you take. If you want it, if you really fucking want it, all you have to do is reach out and grab it."

Matt inhaled a deep breath, was afraid to speak because his goddamned voice would probably shake too much. *It's inside of you, swimming in the marrow of your bones. Pumping through your heart. In each breath you take.*

It was. It always had been. It didn't matter how much he tried to forget it, how much he ignored it. Music would always be sewn into him. He could deny it as much as he wanted but Oliver was right.

So then Matt did exactly what Oliver said. He reached out and took the folder from his hand.

CHAPTER SEVENTEEN

THINGS HAD FELT slightly awkward when Oliver told him he was going to grab a cup of coffee and go get some writing done. Matt almost asked him again if they were okay, if he'd fucked up. Almost told Oliver that he couldn't handle the thought of losing him, but he hadn't.

The truth was, Matt had pulled away from Oliver for years and now here he was, back at Oliver's house when he needed a break from his life. Only now he was fucking him and then wanting to beg him not to let anything change. That was a whole hell of a lot of demands to put on someone. Christ, had he always done that? Had he always orchestrated their relationship that way? Stayed away when he saw fit. Come back when he wanted. Showed up in Oliver's room when he needed him.

So, he'd kept his mouth shut, grabbed his shorts, and slunk out of Oliver's room like he'd just been caught fucking someone he shouldn't have, which was pretty close to the truth.

As Oliver locked himself in his office writing, Matt spent hours in Oliver's spare room going through pages and pages of music. It was amazing to realize how much he'd written, how much time he used to spend with notes and melodies and trying to bring them together into something special.

Matt fingered through the pages, the buzz under his skin getting more and more intense. It was like untapped energy that he hadn't known was there but now it fueled him, made him feel alive in ways he hadn't felt in years.

It was strong enough to carry him downstairs. To make him pull the bench out to the piano for the second time that day. It forced his arms to life and his fingers to move until he played.

Some of the pieces were two frames long while some were pages. Some of them were shit while others made the buzz turn into a riot, into passion and love and beauty that felt like it oozed from his pores, from his fingertips.

His heart beat too hard and too fast. He wanted to laugh. He wanted to cry but he didn't do either of those things. Matt just played—scribbled out old notes he'd written to himself and added new ones. Marked out sections, crumpled papers, added frames.

He breathed again.

For the first time in years, he felt like he could breathe.

"Matt?" He flinched at the sound of Oliver's voice behind him. "I'm sorry to interrupt but it's almost six. I thought you might be getting hungry."

He turned to Oliver just as he approached him. He wore a pair of shorts that he'd put on earlier and a T-shirt.

"It's six?" That was impossible.

"Yeah. I haven't heard you stop in hours so I figured you didn't realize." He paused and then a slow smile tugged at Oliver's lips. "You really got lost in it, didn't you?"

He had. He really fucking had...and it was because of Oliver. He rubbed his hands together because they felt too dry. He'd always had a problem with that, but really, it was just a distraction for himself because he wanted to kiss Oliver, he felt so fucking good.

Instead, Matt asked, "Have you eaten?"

A wrinkle formed above Oliver's brow. "No."

"Come on." Matt forced himself up from the piano. His knees cracked when he did, his legs not wanting to straighten properly; he'd sat on the bench for so long. "I want to make you something to eat." He wasn't sure he could eat, himself. He was too fucking excited, but he wanted to feed Oliver.

Matt made it all the way to the kitchen before Oliver's words stopped him in his tracks. "You have nothing to thank me for."

That was what he'd been trying to do, hadn't he? Thank Oliver for today. Even if it ended now, he...

"You helped me find my music, even if it was only for today."

The same way he had by bringing this piano here, or encouraging Matt to play it when they were younger, or by saving the compositions or getting him into school. He loved Oliver for those things....He always had, but there was a part of him that was ashamed of that—resented Oliver for them as well.

"You give me too much credit. I think you always have," Oliver told him, but Matt didn't see it that way. He maybe wondered if he hadn't given Oliver enough credit for the way he'd always been there for him.

"We'll cook together," Oliver added before he nodded toward the kitchen.

Matt smiled at him, remembering the mess they'd made with the Rice Krispies treats when they were kids....And how much they'd laughed about it afterward. He wanted that again. Their friendship, the way they'd gotten it back at Wild Side last night. "Yeah...I think I can handle that." He was actually looking forward to it.

"I THINK YOU'RE determined to get me fat. I knew you always had it out for me," Matt told him as he mixed eggs in a bowl. His stomach began to growl just being in the kitchen. He glanced up and winked at Oliver who rolled his eyes.

"I'm pretty sure that's not going to be a problem for you. First of all, I remember how much you used to eat and you never had to worry about extra weight. And second, you probably could use some. The bones in your hips dug into my hands earlier."

"Huh?" Matt stopped mixing, set the fork down in the bowl and lifted his shirt. "Do you think I look too skinny?"

Oh, fuck. Now he was going to worry about that. "You're fine." Though a little weight wouldn't hurt him. "Is that something you really worry about or is it because of your job?" he couldn't stop himself from asking before he picked up another potato and began peeling it. He didn't see how mashed potatoes and fried chicken were *that* bad…or maybe he just didn't give a shit about those things.

"A little of both, I guess. Where are your frying pans?"

"Middle cabinet under the island. And why both?"

"Modeling is my livelihood. If I don't work, I don't have money. If I don't look the way they expect me to, I don't work. They go hand in hand. Plus," he shrugged, "and maybe this makes me a pretentious fuck, but…I guess it's important to me to try and look good."

"Pfft." Oliver picked up the colander of potatoes and brought them to the sink to wash them. "I don't think looking good is something you'll ever have to worry about."

"Okay, that's enough of this conversation." Matt had an edge to his voice that he hadn't possessed before. Oliver didn't want to sour the mood, but he also wanted to explore it more deeply.

"Is that really something you worry about? Outside of your job, I mean."

"Yes, Dr. Hayes. I have dreams about it too. The last time I asked, my mirror told me I wasn't the fairest of them all anymore."

Oliver chuckled and accidentally dropped the colander into the sink. Matt was such an anomaly in some ways. Such a contradiction. He resented people focusing on his looks, but he did it himself. "Point taken." Once the potatoes were rinsed, he dumped them into the boiling pot on the stove and made his way back to Matt. Before he could talk himself out of it, he leaned close and said, "I think your mirror is broken, so no poisoned apples, please."

Without looking he knew Matt rolled his eyes. "My life is anything but a fairy tale." He dipped his hand into the bowl of breadcrumbs and damned if he didn't flick a small handful of them at Oliver. They landed half on his face and half in his hair.

"What the hell, Daniels?" Oliver reached for the bowl but Matt blocked him. He put his arms on either side of Matt, trying to fake left and then go right, but Matt didn't fall for it. They were both laughing as he reached out and latched onto Oliver's sides, and tried to move forward as if to use his weight to push Oliver away....But Oliver didn't budge. The only thing it accomplished was lining their bodies up against each other, making them fit together, mold into one another.

Oliver realized his hands weren't on the counter anymore, they were on Matt's arms and he somehow smelled like piano strings.

His cock started to lengthen and Matt's fingers dug into his hips tighter and he really wanted his dick in Matt's ass again. Or his mouth on Matt's cock or his tongue in Matt's mouth or hell, even his tongue in Matt's ass.

"Oliver..." Matt whispered and damned if Oliver didn't shiver.

"Matt..." Oliver countered.

"The water's boiling over."

"Huh?" Oliver ran his hands down Matt's back. Christ, he felt fucking good.

"The water on the stove. It's boiling over."

Oh shit. "Oh shit." Oliver heard the sizzle then. He jerked away from Matt, whipped around and rushed for the stove. Reaching out, he went to turn the stove off just as water splashed out and hit his hand. "Motherfucker," he gritted out before flicking the burner off and pulling the pan off it. His hand stung. His hard-on was gone, and he thought maybe it was a good idea to crawl into the oven and not come out until Matt left. He probably would have if his hand didn't burn so fucking bad.

"Let me see it," Matt said coming up behind him. The skin was red and puffy and stung like a son of a bitch.

"I'm fine." And he felt like an idiot. He'd wanted to bend Matt over the counter and Matt hadn't been thinking anything of the sort.

"Let me see it, Ollie." Matt grabbed his hand and Oliver let him. It was definitely irritated but no blisters. "It looks first degree. Let's get some water on it." He kept hold of Oliver's wrist as though he couldn't make it to the sink alone. From there he turned on the water and put Oliver's hand under the fountain. The coolness immediately started to dull the pain.

Matt didn't let go of him and Oliver didn't pull back. There was obviously no reason why he couldn't do this on his own, but he let Matt hold his hand there. Watched as the water ran over him, ran down his wrist, and cascaded over Matt's hand as well.

Jesus, he was fucking ridiculous. What was it about this man and everything he did that made him come undone like this?

"I think it's okay now." Oliver tried to pull his hand back, but Matt wouldn't let him.

"No. We need to keep it here for three to five minutes."

So they did; they stood there together while their hands were under the cool water. Neither of them spoke, but he noticed Matt watching where their bodies met the same way he did.

"Do you have any aloe or anything?" Matt asked him after minutes ticked by.

"I do. It's in the medicine cabinet in the hall bathroom. I can get it—"

"No." Matt cut him off. "I got it. Keep your hand under the water. I'll be right back."

"Okay," Oliver told him and then did as Matt said. He waited there without moving until Matt came back. When he did it was Matt who turned the water off. Matt who led him to the table where Oliver sat in a chair. Matt who kneeled in front of him and patted his hand dry with a towel. Matt who rubbed the cool aloe onto his skin.

Then he leaned forward and kissed Oliver's wrist before pushing to his feet. "It's not often I get to be the one cleaning up after your silly mistakes. I have to take advantage while I have the chance."

Oliver's chest felt like it began to swell. *Oh, fuck.* Jesus, he was so incredibly screwed because those simple words were a balm to his soul. He'd completely fooled himself if he'd ever thought he could keep himself from getting wrapped up in Matt. The man had entwined himself into Oliver's heart years ago even if it was a mistake for Oliver.

"Looks like I won." Matt shrugged at him, pulling Oliver out of his Matt-trance.

"Huh?"

"I get to make you dinner after all." He reached out and brushed the breadcrumbs out of Oliver's hair.

There was no reason he couldn't continue to help Matt cook, but he didn't move. He just sat there and let Matt do this for him, knowing he needed to.

CHAPTER EIGHTEEN

THEY FELL INTO a routine the next couple of days. Oliver wrote. Matt played and wrote. Playing regularly was only for fun, Matt told himself. Something to do to pass the time while he was there. The truth was, the closer he got to the shoot he'd agreed to do, the more he woke up at night in a cold sweat. The more weight piled onto his chest as he thought about the lights and the cameras and how fucking *on display* he felt during a shoot. Playing Oliver's piano unwound some of the tension inside of him. It made the job feel like it got further away instead of closer.

Maybe it would continue to help. He would need to get another apartment when he got back to New York. Maybe he could get himself a piano and start playing and composing regularly and that would balance out his life, make the noose that had tied itself around his neck in New York loosen.

There were moments in the past couple of days where it didn't feel as though anything was around his throat at all—moments he lost himself to the passion that made him nearly burst at the seams when he played and also spending his evenings cooking with Oliver. That was another part of their new routine. They made dinner together and ate with one another every night. It helped but then Oliver's friendship had always helped. He'd always brought a calmness to Matt's soul.

He stretched before he leaned forward and looked at the music in front of him. Something wasn't right. It sounded rougher...with a bite or an edge to it that Matt wasn't sure felt like him but then every time he tried to soften it, the notes didn't sound right in his head. He wished he had a synthesizer.

Just as he placed his hands on the keys again, his phone rang. Matt closed his eyes, considered ignoring it but then forced himself to look over to see who it was.

Guilt bled through his fingers and would taint what he was doing if he didn't pick it up. He really was an asshole sometimes. "Hey, Mom." They'd spoken a couple of times since he'd been here but he hadn't seen his parents other than that first time.

"Hello. I hope I'm not interrupting..." Her voice trailed off in a way that made Matt shift uncomfortably. He didn't want her to worry about interrupting him. He wanted the kind of relationship Oliver had with his family—for them to feel at ease around each other and to understand each other. It wasn't fair that his mom was caught in the middle of the emotional landmine of his and his father's relationship.

"Of course not. I'm sorry I haven't called or been by to see you again." He took a breath, caressed one of the piano keys with his finger. "How's Dad doing?" Had he made a decision concerning the surgery they hadn't even told him about yet?

"You know your dad—even if he wasn't doing fine, he'd never say it. He's okay, though. We wanted to see if you could make it over for dinner one night before you leave."

He couldn't help but wonder if it was both of them who wanted that or only his mom. Not seeing each other made his relationship with his dad easier. They could both pretend to understand each other, each pretend to be whom the other needed.

"I'd love that. I'll still be here for a while. I have a shoot coming up on Monday." His stomach soured at the words. "I'll be around at least a couple of days after that in case we need reshoots for anything. Maybe we can plan something for then." Would they tell him about the surgery, he wondered? Would his father be able to look him in the eyes?

"That sounds perfect...I...I love you, Matt. We both do. You know that, right?" Her voice was so soft he could hardly hear it but then it echoed inside his head, making him feel a twist of different emotions. Did he know that? Yes. That didn't mean things were easy or cut-and-dried, though. It was hard, feeling as though you didn't fit in with your own family.

"I know, Mom. I love you guys too." When he hung up the phone, Matt immediately pushed off the piano bench and went straight for Oliver's office. He didn't know why but he wanted to see the other man, wanted to talk to him....Was also totally interrupting his work time. Matt lowered his hand just as he was going to knock. Oliver had a job to do. He couldn't drop everything anytime Matt wanted him to.

He got angry that Oliver was always trying to pick up the pieces for him, but then he always went to Oliver when he was falling apart or just wanted someone to talk to. Oliver was always the first person he thought of when something good happened in his life. He was always the first person he thought of when something went wrong as well. That was what he supposed friends were for. It didn't help that ever since they'd fucked, he'd remembered the feel of Oliver's skin. Had Oliver's taste on his tongue and remembered what it was like to have Oliver inside of him.

Christ, he'd almost kissed him in the kitchen before he'd burned himself the other night.

It was a one-off. Something that they didn't need to repeat because eventually, it would screw them, and not in a good way.

It was because he'd always considered himself a sexual creature, he told himself. He enjoyed touching and kissing and fucking. He also enjoyed Oliver so of course, he would continue thinking about putting two of his favorite things into one.

Put two of his favorite things into one? "What the fuck is wrong with me?" Matt whispered to himself and then huffed. It was then that the door pulled open and he realized how close to it he stood. And yes, that he probably looked quite odd creeping around Oliver's office door.

"I heard shuffling around. My mind's not on writing today and I thought maybe I was creating distractions for myself. Why didn't you knock?" Oliver asked.

"I don't know," Matt replied. "Do you wanna get out of here?"

"Yeah," Oliver told him. "Yeah, I do."

***

THEY DECIDED TO hike Runyon Canyon. They hadn't gone together since one of Matt's early visits years ago, and it was something they'd both always enjoyed. They changed clothes and called a cab because it was hell trying to park.

Oliver hadn't been lying when he said he'd been restless. Then he'd heard the movement outside his door and had known that Matt felt the same but that he likely wouldn't come in. It would be too needy for Matt and well, Oliver was the opposite. When he felt something, he wanted to grab on, to show the world how he felt. It was funny how differently they could be built, but it didn't change the strength of their friendship.

They'd just gotten out of the cab at Runyon when Oliver felt a nudge to his arm. He looked over at Matt who had an ear-to-ear smile on his face. It was really incredible when Matt looked truly happy about something. Still, Oliver knew looks could be deceiving.

"I'm excited," Matt told him.

"To hike Runyon?" He knew that was what Matt meant so he wasn't sure why he'd asked.

"Yes. The first time I ever hiked Runyon was with you."

Oliver pushed his hands into his pockets. "Yeah…yeah, I remember. It was me, you and Chance."

"No," Matt told him. "That was the second time. The first it was just you and me. We'd been at your house. I had a shitty day. I think my dad pissed me off and you brought me. Don't you remember?"

The memory came flooding back to him. How in the hell had he forgotten? It wasn't often that Oliver let memories slip away. "Oh yeah," Oliver replied. "You stepped in a hole and twisted your ankle. I practically had to carry you down." Jesus, that had been a fun day.

"What? It wasn't that bad! I hobbled on my own quite nicely."

Okay, so maybe he'd exaggerated a little bit but it was more fun that way. "You *did* have your arm around me and I *did* take some of your weight."

"My ankle was swollen!" Matt countered with a smile.

"See? So I saved the day. I like to pretend I'm the knight in shining armor sometimes." Which was likely, not really a good thing and the sometimes was really always.

"You are," Matt told him quietly as they began making their way up the trail. The sun was high in the sky and beating down on them, but there was a light breeze that kept the heat from being unbearable. His favorite thing about growing up in Southern California had always been the weather.

The look on Matt's face changed, the set of his shoulders a little more serious when he admitted, "You always save the day. That's why I had to leave."

Discomfort slid down Oliver's spine. Yes, he knew Matt felt like he needed to do things on his own but to hear him say the words the way he just did made his muscles seize up. As if he sensed how Oliver felt, Matt added, "I didn't mean that the way it sounded. I left because of me and only me. You didn't drive me away. I needed to go but…you're the glue that holds everyone together, Ollie. You have to know that. You're exactly who Miles needs you to be and exactly who Chance needs you to be. You're the same with me and it would have been too easy to let you continue to be my savior. It would have been too easy for you to continue doing it because your heart doesn't work any other way."

Oliver's gut suddenly felt heavy, his feet like he was trying to walk through thick mud. "Why does that sometimes feel like a bad thing?" he asked as he made his way around some brush. Chance had never understood him—his need to be there for people. He didn't give Oliver a lot of shit for who he was, but he didn't *get* him. Miles made him feel like he should change who he was. He knew his friend didn't mean for it to sound that way but it's how Oliver often felt. And Matt? Matt had run away from him.

The fact that he cared seemed to be the core of a lot of the strife in his life.

"It's not."

"Isn't it, though?" he asked. It wasn't as if his heart had done him much good. It was more like his heart was a liability.

"Come on. You know better than that."

Maybe he did but still, he didn't respond. He didn't know how to respond. There was no changing who he was and he also couldn't change how people felt about that. He wouldn't apologize for giving a shit about people, either.

They were silent for a few moments as they continued to climb the canyon. It was quieter here than it often was. There was no one directly behind or in front of them, but he did hear a dog bark in the distance. It was a popular place to walk pets.

Finally, Matt spoke again. "It's not a bad thing, okay? It's not and…I think part of me wanted to make you proud….I'm not sure if I realized it until later but I guess…" Oliver stopped moving, couldn't make himself take another step as he listened to Matt. He stopped too, looked at Oliver and added, "I guess you always believed in me so much; you put yourself on the line for me so much—getting me into school and becoming my friend—I wanted you to see it was worth it. I wanted you to know you didn't put all that energy out in vain."

Oliver's heart beat wildly against his chest. His hands got sweaty so he pulled them out of his pockets, Matt's words a constant echo in his brain. *I think part of me wanted to make you proud....I guess you always believed in me so much; you put yourself on the line for me so much; I wanted you to see it was worth it. I wanted you to know you didn't put all that energy out in vain.*

"I would never think that. You have to know that. Christ, Matt. I've always loved you just the way you are. You don't ever have to work to make me proud."

Matt paused, looking down, but then Oliver hooked his finger beneath Matt's chin and tilted his head back up so they were looking each other in the eyes. "Are you hearing me?"

"Yes, sir." Matt winked at him but Oliver didn't take the bait.

"I'm serious."

He sighed. "I know you are. And I get it, I do. It's just the brain and the heart aren't always in sync."

That, Oliver definitely understood because his brain had told him to stop loving Matt years ago, but his damn heart wouldn't accept the truth.

It was then that Oliver realized he was leaning forward. Nothing could hold him back this time as his lips got closer to Matt's. There was no boiling pot to distract them. The earth would have to open up and swallow him whole to keep Oliver from kissing Matt this time.

"Why do we keep ending up like this?" Matt whispered.

"Don't know," Oliver replied, but he did. This is what he'd always wanted. Matt was always what he'd wanted.

When his mouth pressed against Matt's, his friend immediately parted his lips for him. Their tongues danced, tangled together. He still had his finger beneath Matt's chin. He slid it over, placing his hand on Matt's neck as he pulled him closer, kissed him deeper. He tasted like adventure—adventure and passion and history, and Oliver wanted to savor it. Wanted to know that taste better than he knew anything else.

Matt's hands went to his hips as he kissed Oliver back with everything Oliver gave him. When they finally pulled away, he asked a question that had been on his mind for a couple of days now. "Do you want to go to the symphony on Friday night? I asked my dad and he was able to score us tickets. I know you love going."

Matt cocked his head, his stare intensely on Oliver. He felt it to the marrow of his bones even though he didn't know what it meant.

"What about Wild Side with Chance and Miles?"

"I can miss one night," Oliver told him. They never missed a Friday night, but he would.

"I…yeah…I'd love to go. Will you go with me? To my shoot on Monday? Will you go?"

He'd always wanted to see Matt in action. Always wanted to support him that way but in that moment, it sounded important to Matt. Almost like he needed it. "Of course." He winked at Matt and backed up, breaking the trance they were in. "Now, come on. Let's finish this hike unless you're scared you can't hack it. I don't want to have to carry you down again."

Matt laughed. "Fuck you. I'm like a hiking champion now."

"When is the last time you hiked anything?" He cocked a brow.

"Not important," Matt replied, and then they finished their hike.

CHAPTER NINETEEN

MATT WAS NERVOUS. He had no reason to be. This was Oliver he was going out with and Oliver's parents would be there, for Christ's sake, but something about this felt different from all the times they'd spent time together throughout their lives. As though it meant more, wasn't just two friends hanging out.

Maybe it was the fact that they'd fucked. It had always been important to him to keep those lines neatly drawn where Oliver was concerned and first the sex, then that fucking kiss he'd given Matt at Runyon had made his toes curl and his dick hard all in one.

This was a mistake.

It could turn out really fucking bad.

But there was no way he couldn't go.

It might not seem like it, but Oliver skipping a Friday at Wild Side was a big deal. He didn't let people down. It wasn't how he worked and he would see skipping the night as letting Miles and Chance down.

And he was doing it for Matt.

His chest seized up, constricting around his heart. How did he get so lucky as to get this man in his life? To have his friendship for all these years?

And he hadn't always been a good friend to Oliver in return. That was the thought that hadn't left his head for days.

"Knock, knock." Oliver's voice came softly from the doorway. "You okay? You're spacing out over there."

Matt stood in front of the window as Oliver came through the open door. Matt's heart sped up while a low twist also tied his stomach into knots. There was something he needed to say and he'd waited too long to do it.

"I'm sorry," he said, not looking at Oliver.

"For what? You're not canceling on me, are you?" he asked. Matt could tell he tried to sound playful but there was a real hint of worry lacing his voice. It made him feel even shittier that he'd given Oliver reasons to expect that over the years.

"No, I'm not canceling. I just…" He sighed. "I've never apologized for leaving the way I did, have I? For leaving you hanging and not telling you beforehand that I planned to go to New York."

Without looking at Oliver, Matt knew he had a puzzled look on his face. He was the kind of man who wouldn't expect or need an apology, but he deserved one.

"It was over ten years ago, Matty. It doesn't matter."

At that, Matt turned his way. Oliver looked gorgeous, his dark blond hair recently trimmed and neat. He wore a gray suit. It hugged him in all the right places, and suddenly he felt the urge to tug on the bow tie at Oliver's neck and pull him closer.

He shook those thoughts from his head. "It does matter how long it's been. You were my best friend. You *are* my best friend, and I kept something from you that hurt you. I lied to you and I did it on purpose. We both know that's not the only thing I have to apologize to you for—springing the blond on you my first visit. Fuck, I can't even remember the kid's name." But he'd brought the guy on purpose because he'd been alone, so fucking alone in New York without his friends. Without Oliver. Because he'd hit brick wall after brick wall, and he'd been scared to death if he didn't come with a line of defense, he would have stayed in Los Angeles. "The missing trips, not calling, only calling when it suited me. There's so much I owe you an apology for. I've been a horrible friend to you,

Ollie and I'm sorry. When I leave, when I go back to New York, I promise you, things will be different."

And they would be. Matt would be different. He would be better.

"Hey, it's okay. You and me? We're good, Matty. Always." Oliver wrapped an arm around Matt and pulled him close. He kissed Matt's forehead, and Matt tucked his face into Oliver's neck. He wasn't sure what had hit him all of a sudden, why he had to make sure Oliver knew he was sorry and how much their friendship meant to him. Probably because he knew Oliver deserved better. He deserved better than how most people treated him—even Miles and Chance, but especially Matt himself.

When they pulled away, Oliver pushed Matt's hair off his forehead. They stood less than a foot apart, facing each other. "You look good. Not that I'm surprised."

Matt wore a suit as well, but his was a dark blue.

"Thanks. You don't clean up so badly, yourself. Your bow tie is crooked. Let me fix it for you."

So he did. His hands shook, he noticed, as he raised them toward his friend. Oliver closed his eyes while Matt straightened his bow tie. Matt dropped his hands when he finished. Oliver's lids slid open and he nodded toward the door. "Let's get out of here, Matty."

Matt smiled, an uncertainty he wasn't used to working its way through his system.

"It'll be good to see your parents," he told Oliver as they were in the car on their way to the restaurant. They were just like Oliver in so many ways. They could have easily looked down on Matt but they never had. They'd treated him like a son, and he would forever be grateful for that.

"They're excited to see you as well. Mom was surprised she hadn't thought of getting the tickets for us to join them tonight."

Matt wasn't surprised that Oliver had thought of it. Not that he wouldn't expect Ralph or Vivian Hayes to consider it because they would as well, but Oliver? This was all him—giving someone who was important to him something that would make them happy.

He reached over and squeezed Oliver's knee. "I haven't been in a long time. I'm glad it's you that I'm going with."

Oliver glanced his way, a small frown tugging at his lips that Matt didn't understand. He turned away before Matt could comment on it—or at least, Matt told himself that he shouldn't.

"No problem. It's nice to do something different."

When they arrived at the restaurant, Oliver dropped off the car with the valet and they made their way inside. Ralph and Viv were already seated at a table in the upscale restaurant right down the street from the symphony.

As soon as Viv saw them, she pushed to her feet and covered her mouth with her hands.

"She's a little excited," Oliver teased but for Matt, a warmth spread through him, settling in his chest while at the same time he felt guilty because of it. He had his own parents who loved him with all their hearts. But it was different with Oliver's family. They'd always accepted the boys for who they were, always understood them in a way his own family struggled with.

"Matt Daniels, I cannot believe it has been so many years since we've seen you. If I weren't such a respectable woman, I'd kick your butt!"

She smiled a smile that was just like Oliver's. Her hair was lighter in color than Oliver's, but he looked a lot more like his mom than his dad, who was a beefy man.

The second Viv opened her arms, Matt stepped into them. "I know. I'm sorry," he said as he hugged her. And he was. He hadn't done right by anyone back home—not Oliver's parents, Oliver, or even his own family. "It won't happen again."

"You bet your ass it won't!" she replied before letting him go.

"Oh, hey, Oliver. I didn't see you there," she teased, and Matt heard his friend laugh.

"You're a real comedienne, Mom."

"Come here, you," she told her son just before Oliver went in to hug her.

Matt said his hellos to Ralph next, followed by Oliver, and then they sat at the table.

They asked Matt about his life in New York. Viv teased about seeing him in his underwear in a magazine, and that he needed to keep his clothes on. They laughed. Told Matt how proud of him they were before they spoke about their son and all he'd accomplished.

"We're so proud of all four of our boys," Viv said. "You're all such good men and have done so many wonderful things."

Had they, though? What had Matt done except use his face and distance himself from people he loved?

"I have to admit, you've broken my heart a little bit, though."

Matt's eyes shot toward Viv at that.

"Mom," Oliver warned.

"Yes. You have that correct, Ollie. I'm the mom which means I'm allowed to say these things, and Matt will write it off as sappy things a mother says." She turned her attention back to Matt. "We miss you. I understand, but I wish you didn't have to go so far away. There was a part of me that always thought I'd be able to really call you my son one day."

Matt had taken a sip of his wine just as she'd spoken. He coughed as it went down the wrong tube and nearly choked on it.

Oliver chuckled while he patted Matt on the back.

"I always thought you would end up with Oliver one day. Matt, your mother and I used to talk about it."

"You did?" he asked, hearing the surprise in his own voice. His mom had thought that about him and Oliver? It wasn't something they'd ever talked about—Matt's future. If he would get married or have a family.

"Oh yes. I think she was surprised when I mentioned it. She didn't realize Oliver had a little crush on you back in high school."

"Ma. Really?" Oliver interrupted and Viv just winked at him.

"Anyway. I told her and she was happy. She worries about you, Matt. She's like all other moms out there, and she just wants her baby to be happy."

It wasn't his mom he'd been as worried about as his father.

"Anyway. You know I love your family, and I thought we would all be one *big* family one day. I guess Ralph was right about this one, and the two of you were only meant to be friends."

Matt turned to look at Oliver then. He gave Matt a small shrug and looked away as Viv continued. "Now, if my son doesn't hurry up and find himself a good boy, I'm going to have to find one for him. Are you dating, Oliver?"

"Do we really have to do this right now?" Oliver asked, and apparently they did. Viv, Ralph, and their son went back and forth about Oliver, dating, his being their only kid, and she wanted to plan a wedding, *damn it.* The whole time, Matt just watched Oliver. Thought about him finding someone. About him settling down and sharing his home with another man, and how whoever it was would be the luckiest guy on earth.

Discomfort pricked at the base of his spine, making him shift in his seat.

When they finished the conversation, Oliver took a bite of his food, then another. He looked Matt's way with a small frown on his full lips. "You're not eating your food. Does it not taste good? We can get you something else."

Matt shook his head. "My stomach is a little upset. I think it's all the excitement. I'll be fine."

Oliver didn't reply, and he didn't look away. Matt had to be the one to break the eye contact first.

CHAPTER TWENTY

ATT'S BODY TREMBLED from the inside out—the epicenter a burst of energy and passion that he thought he'd combust trying to contain. Tears danced at the end of his eyelashes, but he was too engrossed in the scene in front of him, in the music floating through him to take the time to brush them away. Music was love and desire and happiness—everything beautiful in the world. That was the way it made him feel.

In that moment, as he watched the composer direct musicians, as he listened to passion flow from every instrument, he felt almost whole. It wasn't often he felt that way. Without taking his eyes away from the scene in front of him, he let his hand drift over to Oliver who sat beside him. He threaded their fingers together, needing some kind of contact with his best friend. With Oliver.

He squeezed Matt's hand and held it while they listened. It felt like only seconds had passed by when the symphony ended. People moved around them, got out of their seats and talked about how beautiful the night had been, but Matt still couldn't move. He heard Oliver tell his parents they would be a few moments and his parents saying they would talk to them another day.

Oliver continued to hold Matt's hand and he let him. Minutes passed by. The space around them completely emptied out. Oliver didn't speak, didn't even shift, just gave Matt the time he needed.

"Thank you," he finally managed to say.

"You have nothing to thank me for," Oliver told him, but he

did. Matt felt like he could never thank Oliver enough for everything he had given him. He didn't know where to start. He felt too raw, like everything inside of him was on display for the world to see. It was always so damn hard to understand his own emotions—how he could appreciate the things Oliver did but then other times, they made him feel incapable of doing things for himself. How sometimes he could want to pull Oliver closer but others he needed to push him away.

"Will you take me home now?" Matt asked.

"Yeah…yeah, of course. Come on. Let's go." Oliver stood and led the way out, still holding onto Matt's hand.

It was strange, how he didn't remember getting home, but the next thing he knew they were walking into Oliver's house and he was asking, "Can I go to your room with you?" There was no weight to his voice, no meat to it, just bare bones, honest and raw.

"As long as you're going because that's where you want to be, even if it's only for tonight and not because you feel like you owe me something."

"Come on, Ollie. You know me better than that. There are a lot of promises I can't make you—I don't know what this means, or why I need it, but I've always been a selfish bastard. I'm not having sex with you because I owe you something; I'm having sex with you because I want to. Because I need you, and that's not easy for me to admit."

Oliver gave him a slow nod, and the two men made their way up the stairs. The earthquake inside of Matt hadn't subsided. It was as if the reason transitioned from music to Oliver.

He was surprised when Oliver went straight for the bathroom. When he turned on the water in his glass-enclosed shower.

Oliver's fingers went to Matt's tie, but Matt stopped him. "No…let me take care of you. You're always the one taking care of me."

A haze bled into Oliver's eyes, but he gave a quick nod, and then Matt got to work. He pulled the tie loose, pushed the jacket off Oliver's shoulders. From there he slowly worked each of the buttons on his shirt. As he revealed Oliver's skin, he leaned forward, kissing his way down Oliver's chest, twirling his tongue around each nipple, nibbling at his collarbone.

"Oh, fuck," rasped past Oliver's lips as he dropped his head back. Matt paid more attention to Oliver's throat, licking and sucking on his salty flesh until Oliver's shirt was completely open, and he could drop that to the floor next.

Matt's jacket and tie went right after, followed by his shirt. He lowered down to his knees, lifted Oliver's foot—first one and then the other, removing his shoes.

"What are you doing?" Oliver asked.

"Fixing a car," Matt replied, making the other man chuckle. "Undressing you. What do you think I'm doing?" After Oliver's shoes, he went for his socks, then opened his pants and began pulling them and his black underwear down his legs.

Oliver's thick cock burst free, and Matt leaned forward, circling the head with his tongue. "If I would have known you were packing this, we might have started fucking years ago." He leaned in and nuzzled Oliver's balls. He'd always had a thing for having his face between a man's legs but as he rubbed his nose against Oliver's sac before tonguing it, he thought he could spend even more time here, kneeling for Oliver, and memorizing every inch of this spot on the man.

"Christ, Matt. You're killing me. You look so goddamned beautiful down there." Oliver's hand tightened in his hair as he pushed Matt's face closer to him and Matt took advantage, sucking his balls, taking in his scent and running his tongue up and down Oliver's impressive shaft.

"That's enough for now," Oliver said and pulled him to his feet.

He liked the way Oliver took control in the bedroom. He was passive other ways in his life but here, he liked to be the one to run things, and Matt liked letting him.

Oliver disposed of Matt's clothes faster than Matt had his, and then they were in the shower, kissing beneath the spray. Oliver lifted him, pressed Matt's back against the wall and Matt wrapped his legs around his waist.

He ran a hand over Matt's ribcage and pulled far enough away to say, "You're too skinny."

"I've always been small," he replied and he had, but Oliver also knew he was a whole lot thinner than he had been in high school.

"You're too small, Matt, and you know it." Oliver's mouth went down on his again. They kissed and rubbed against each other until Oliver put him down. "This tattoo is so fucking sexy." He rubbed the ink on Matt's hip.

There was soap next…and more kissing. As much as Matt enjoyed it, he felt like he would be eviscerated with desire if Oliver didn't fuck him soon.

As if he'd read Matt's thoughts, the water turned off, and they were drying themselves before Oliver pulled him to the bed. He cupped Matt's ass, spread his cheeks and with his face close to Matt's ear he said, "I want my face right there, Matt. Wanna taste your hole before I'm inside it."

A tremor rocked through him. Matt bucked his hips, wanting just that. "I love being rimmed."

"You'll love it even more by me."

"Oooh. When did you get so cocky?"

"When I landed Matt Daniels."

Matt didn't have a chance to think about those words because Oliver was manhandling him, flipping him to his stomach, Matt's face in the pillows. He lay between Matt's spread legs and ran his tongue from the base of Matt's spine down his crack.

A strangled moan ripped from Matt's throat as he thrust, rubbing his cock against the bed.

Oliver palmed his cheeks, then spread them. "Christ, this fucking hole, Matty. It's so goddamned perfect. So tight. I could eat it and fuck it all day."

That sounded perfect to Matt. "Then do it," he said. That was all Oliver needed to go at him, tonguing Matt's asshole—fast then slow. He used his teeth on Matt's ass cheeks. Spit on his pucker then fingered it, sliding the digit in and out while he flicked it with his tongue until Matt thought he would lose his fucking mind.

Rolling wave after wave washed over him. His hands fisted in the blankets. He pumped his hips, needing friction on his cock, his body shattering bit by bit as Oliver rubbed his prostate.

"Please...I need you. I need your dick in me."

Then Oliver was gone. There was fumbling in the bedside drawer and Matt knew he was getting a condom and lube. He heard the package rip open, saw Oliver's hands shake as he rolled the condom down his leaking erection before he rubbed lube on himself.

The cold was a shock to Matt's system when Oliver squirted it onto his asshole, rubbing it in before he said, "Get up. I want you to ride me."

Yeah...yeah, Matt wanted that too.

Matt moved, and then Oliver lay in the middle of the bed. Matt straddled him, grabbed Oliver's hot erection, rubbing it on himself before he slid down on it. Oliver's hands were on his waist, his blunt nails digging into Matt's skin as they breathed together while Matt filled himself with Oliver's cock.

He looked down, saw so much fucking emotion in Oliver's eyes it nearly took his breath. His pulse sped up and he nearly ran. Jesus, the way Oliver looked at him. It made Matt feel like he was someone else. Someone better. Someone he could never be. Oliver had always seen more in him than was there.

Obviously sensing Matt's warring emotions, Oliver said, "No. Fuck that, Matt. Don't run because you see something you don't want to see. I don't deserve that and neither do you. I'm a big boy. I know what I'm doing."

Oh God. What if he fucked up? What if he hurt Oliver? What if he lost him?

"Ride me, babe. Show me how you can work that ass. I want it. Christ, I fucking want it so much."

He wanted it too. He always had, in his own way. He'd always wanted to be a part of Oliver like this. Always wanted to know Oliver this way, even if he knew he wasn't what Oliver really needed. Oliver had to know that as well.

But this? This Matt could give him.

He leaned forward, taking Oliver's mouth as the fat cock inside him slid almost all the way out before Matt sat on him again. He kept that going, riding Oliver the way Oliver told him to. Each time their bodies met, Oliver hit his prostate just right.

A guttural growl ripped from Oliver's throat and Matt was proud to be the one to pull those sounds out of him, to drive him so wild.

The faster he went, the more Oliver's nails dug into him, the faster he breathed and the thicker he felt stretching out Matt's hole.

He looked down just as a thin rope of pre-come leaked from his cock and pooled on Oliver's belly. The other man wiped it with his finger, licked it, then spit in his hand and started to stroke Matt as he rode him.

"Oh, fuck…*fuck*." Matt dropped his head back, closed his eyes as he bounced on Oliver's cock, his skillful hand on his dick just the addition he needed.

"Jesus, I'm going to come. I'm going to fucking come, Ollie."

"That's the point," he said, amusement and lust in his voice.

The greedy pulls on his erection got faster. The build-up in Matt's body higher and higher until he couldn't keep it contained anymore. He leaned back farther, grabbed Oliver's legs as he fucked himself on Oliver's dick.

His balls let loose, some of the tension in Matt's body seeping out as he shot his load all over Oliver's hand.

"Look at me, Matt," Oliver said softly as another pulse of come ran down Oliver's hand.

Matt looked down at him, looked him in the eyes before Oliver pulled him closer. Before he took Matt's mouth and pistoned in and out of him. He held Matt in place, mouths fused together, ass in the perfect spot for Oliver to fuck, his hips jackhammering as he thrust into Matt's ass in rapid speed. He kept going, kept thrusting until Oliver went rigid. Until he roughly called out Matt's name as he came.

Oliver sat up, wrapped his arms around Matt, sticky come between them…and he let Oliver hold him. Savored the feel of their skin sticking together. Of Oliver's hand on his ass and his arm around Matt's back. Matt held onto Oliver too, needing the contact. He dropped his head back and looked up because this felt right in a way that scared the shit out of him.

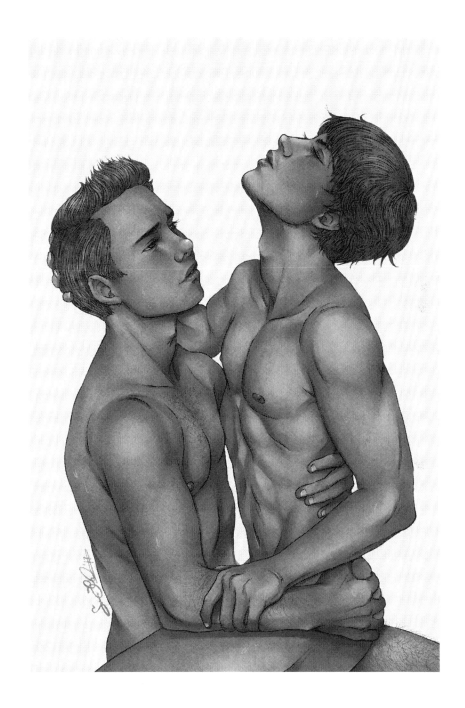

CHAPTER TWENTY-ONE

M ATT STILL STRADDLED him and Oliver let his fingers trail up and down Matt's back. They dipped in each of the ridges of his spine and ran across the sharp edges at the points. He didn't like how skinny Matt was. He'd always been a slender man but he used to have more meat on his bones than he did now.

There was a quiet worry in the back of his head, one he was afraid to voice out loud that wondered if this was a problem for Matt. If eating was a problem for him. During the time he'd been here, he'd picked a lot, pushed food around his plate, but then he'd indulge in mammoth bowls of cereal with him so maybe he was overreacting.

"I'll be right back. I need to get rid of the condom." Matt leaned his head down and Oliver kissed his forehead. Then he turned slightly, set Matt on the bed and got out from under him. He pulled the condom off as he went, tying it while he walked to the bathroom and threw it into the trash. He turned the faucet on, rinsed his hands and tossed some water on his face. He grabbed a towel from the rack and dried himself because he felt like he needed to do something, to move and keep busy.

As he walked back to his room, he noticed Matt's eyes intensely on him.

"You're really beautiful, Ollie. Do you know that?" he said. Oliver rolled his eyes as he climbed back into the bed. He paused for a second before he wrapped and arm around Matt and pulled him close so his head rested on Oliver's chest.

"Thanks, but you're the beautiful one. Not me. Everyone knows it."

Matt groaned, the sound vibrating through Oliver but then he said, "We can both be beautiful."

There was doubt there, in the roughness of his voice. In the way the tone dropped an octave. Oliver recognized the sound. "You don't really believe it, do you?" he asked. How could he not? How could Matt not see how gorgeous he was?

"Oh, fuck. Let's not do this. I didn't say that for you to turn this around to me." He tried to move but Oliver kept ahold of him, tightening his grip. Matt didn't fight him.

"I'm serious," he said, before tilting Matt's head up so he looked at him.

"You're always trying to make other people feel good. My statement was supposed to be about you."

"You're always trying to deflect. You know I'm good at getting my way. I won't stop until you give it to me."

Matt's brows pulled together, a little wrinkle forming on his forehead. "Isn't that me?"

"Fuck, you're right." Oliver laughed because he knew Matt needed him to, but then he went quiet, and he knew Matt also understood he wouldn't drop this.

"Christ, Ollie. I just came so hard my ears are ringing; do we have to do this right now?"

Pride surged through him at knowing he'd driven Matty so far out of his fucking mind. But still…

"I have to take advantage post-orgasm. It's my only chance."

Matt grabbed Oliver's cock. "How about I get you hard again and suck you off instead?"

Damned if there wasn't a part of him that really liked that idea, but the stronger part of him felt this was too important. "Tell me you know you're fucking beautiful, Matty. I need to hear it."

Matt sighed, flopped to his back and threw an arm over his eyes. "Of course I know I'm attractive. I see it when I look in the mirror. People tell me all the fucking time. *You're beautiful, Matt. Your skin…your cheekbones…*on and fucking on. *Be careful, Matt, you don't want to lose what you have going for you.*"

The last one made Oliver's body go rigid. Made his ears ring but not from his orgasm the way Matt had said his did. "Who in the fuck said that to you?"

Matt sat up, his back against the headboard. "Don't be naïve, Ollie. Nearly everyone has said those words to me. It's part of my job. I have nothing without my looks and my body."

Oliver's vision went blurry. His body went hot. "Fuck whoever said that to you. You're more than your job; let's get that out of the way first. Modeling isn't who you are. Second, you're a whole hell of a lot more than what you look like. You're smart. Loyal. Passionate. Kind."

Matt shook his head, but Oliver kept going.

"You're funny. You think of others. You make people feel good by being around them. You're a better musician than I am a writer. You—"

"Then why couldn't I make it?" Matt's words came out sharp, a bite to them that stung Oliver's heart. And then, more quietly, he repeated, "Why couldn't I make it, Ollie?"

Oliver's hands shook. His heart broke. He'd wondered, all these years he'd wondered about Matt and his music. "You listen to me." When Matt didn't look at him, Oliver grabbed him, pulled him over so he straddled Oliver and couldn't look away. "What happened to you?"

"I woke up," Matty said softly. "I fucking knew, *knew* that I was going to go to New York and all my dreams were going to come true. People would be begging for me. I was going to do it and I was going to do it on my own."

That last part was for Oliver, but it didn't hurt. It just made him respect Matt for wanting to make his own way.

"There's not a big story if that's what you're looking for here. I was young, naïve. I guess I thought because I wanted it so fucking much, because I sacrificed for it, that it would happen. I was broke, working two, sometimes three jobs. I was a little fish in a big fucking ocean. I was still nothing special. I couldn't get anyone to give me the time of day until I met the guy who got me my first modeling gig. *Fuck music. You're too pretty for that shit. Use what you have,* he told me, so I did. Turns out he just wanted his dick in my ass and then I met Parker, and he was real. I used my face and it got me further than my talent ever could." There was defiance in Matt's voice, in the set of his body and the way he looked at Oliver, but he knew sadness lived underneath. Sadness that wanted to pull Matty under and hell, maybe it had.

Maybe Matt had been drowning for years and Oliver had never realized it.

"You're more than your looks," Oliver reiterated.

"Am I?" he asked back.

Oliver cupped Matt's cheek, rubbed his thumb across it. "I love you...*you* and not because of how you look or what you do for a living. I love you and I know you know it. You've always known it, haven't you?"

Matt sucked in a sharp breath, then closed his eyes and leaned into Oliver's hand. It was as if he could only give himself that one second—and then he was opening his eyes and slightly pulling his face away from Oliver's hand until he dropped it.

"You want to take care of me, Ollie. Want to fix me, to help me. There's a difference."

Oliver's insides damn near turned to stone. "Fuck you, Matt." He tried to move but this time it was Matt stopping him. Matt's hand on his chest, as he didn't budge from Oliver's lap.

"You deserve better than me," Matt added.

"Fuck you if you think that, too. Those are excuses and you know it. It's okay that you don't feel the same. I've always known you don't, but don't patronize me. Don't tell me how I *should* feel or how I *do* feel or make excuses. You don't love me and that's it. Say it."

Matt didn't speak, didn't move. Both men breathed heavily, their chests rapidly moving in and out, their breaths mixing. Finally, after what felt like a lifetime, Matt said, "I'm afraid to feel the same way."

Oliver's pulse rapped against his skin. He swallowed around the tension in his throat. "I would never hurt you."

The sad look in Matt's eyes told him that wasn't what he was afraid of. He was afraid he would hurt Oliver. "You give me shit for trying to take care of you, for trying to protect you, but you do the same fucking thing to me."

They were at an impasse. Oliver knew that. Neither of them would budge...but he felt better knowing that he'd spoken his truth. That he'd told Matt how he felt. Maybe then when Matt left, he would finally be able to move on.

"I should go back to my room," Matt said but didn't move.

"Don't be stupid. We're grown-ass men. We fucked, not for the first time, remember? We both know that's all this is. Lie down and go to sleep, Matty. We had a good night. I don't want to ruin it now."

Matt nodded and climbed off him. He lay on his side, his back toward Oliver. He watched Matt for a moment, then turned out the light and curled up behind him, with his arm around Matt's waist. He let his finger dance up and down Matty's ribcage.

"Do you have an eating disorder, Matt?" He held his breath as he waited for an answer.

"You've seen me eat."

"Not what I asked."

He sighed. "I'm fine. Again, I've always been thin. I have a shoot coming up and a lot of shit on my mind, which makes me lose my appetite. I'm fine. I promise you, I'm fine." He paused, "Are you still going to go?"

"Of course. You know I won't let you down." Oliver squeezed him tighter and hoped like hell they were going to be okay.

CHAPTER TWENTY-TWO

OLIVER KNEW HE needed to go see Miles. He would be pissed about last night, there were no two ways about it. He would take Oliver going with Matt on Friday night as Oliver being too wrapped up in Matt, and maybe he was right. The thing was, he didn't feel you could be too much of anything when it came to Matt, which was another red flag that Miles would call him on if he voiced it.

He'd left his house around the same time as Matt today, the other man having some kind of work thing he had to do for his upcoming shoot.

He was let into Miles's building and took the elevator up to his apartment. The second he made it to the door, it was pulled open by his friend. Miles didn't have a shirt on, his brown skin slightly sweaty as though he'd been working out. "Manage to squeeze me into your schedule, did you?"

Oh yeah. He was pissed. Oliver wasn't the least bit surprised. "It was one fucking night. Don't act like that. You're being childish." Oliver stepped inside. He'd always thought Miles's apartment was slightly cold. It was mostly done in grays and blues—a lot of stainless steel and even steel artwork—very modern.

It was open concept with a bar on the edge of the kitchen, the living room on the other side. Oliver headed for that room and sat on the black couch.

"You're sleeping with him, aren't you?" was the first thing Miles asked.

Fuck. He should have known the other man would see it. When Oliver didn't answer Miles groaned out, *"Jesus."*

"What is your issue with him? Christ, Miles. You act like he's not one of us. Like we haven't been friends with him for years. You're the one always telling me to get laid, so I did. Why do you give a shit who I fuck?"

"Because we're friends!" He shook his head. "I've known you and Chance my entire fucking life. We've always said there would never be any fucking between any of us, and the second Matt came around you wanted him. What happens when he breaks your heart, Ollie? Then that brings unrest between all of us. And if he doesn't…then shit like last night happens. It fucks with our core. You know you're the heart of this group."

Oliver closed his eyes, the weight of twenty-eight years of friendship suddenly on his chest. He should have seen this before. Why hadn't he seen it before? He opened his eyes and looked at Miles, as the other man gave him his back. Miles knew he would speak and Oliver knew it would be easier for Miles if he didn't look at Oliver while he did it.

"Nothing will ever change our friendship. You know that. Not Matt or anyone else. I love you. Chance loves you. Hell, Matty loves you too. We won't walk away from you. I know that because—"

"Stop." Miles cut him off. "I'm not going to do this. Just…just be careful. I'm not worried about me. I'm worried about you."

There wasn't a part of Oliver that didn't believe that. "Maybe you should start worrying about yourself a little more."

At that, Miles turned back toward him and rolled his deep, brown eyes. "Don't start to psychoanalyze me. I'm just trying to protect that big squishy heart of yours."

Oliver chuckled. "It's not squishy."

"It's a little squishy." Miles walked over. They sat on the couch. Miles leaned against the back of it. "So you finally got yourself a piece of Matt's ass. Was it as good as you thought it would be?"

There was zero surprise Miles had asked him that. "I'm not answering that." He felt his face heat.

"You're blushing. Holy Christ, you're blushing. It must be even better than you hoped for."

The two of them laughed, and it felt good to have the tension between them dissolve. It had been there ever since Matt called and said he was coming back. When they settled down, Miles turned his head toward Oliver. "Did you tell him you're in love with him?"

Oliver's throat began to tighten. The pressure radiated down to his chest. "He knows. You were right; he's always known."

"I—" Miles started but his voice cracked. He swallowed and then continued, "I think he's just afraid of being hurt. It's not you but that's still not fair *to* you. Fear makes people do a lot of shit, and I don't want you to get caught in the results." Miles reached over and squeezed Oliver's knee.

He wondered how much Miles's own fears held him back or how often he got caught in his own trap. "I know, man. I know."

They spent the next little while talking about Friday night—both his evening with Chance at Wild Side and Oliver and Matt at the symphony. He told Miles that Matt was composing again but that he wasn't sure how long it would last.

Miles listened and wished Matt the best. Oliver had a feeling that the music wouldn't last and soon, Matt would be back in New York, distancing himself from his life in Los Angeles again.

"YOU LOOK BETTER than you did when you first came home," Matt's mom said as they stood in the kitchen doing dishes together. He'd come over and had dinner with them tonight, deciding it was better before his shoot than after. It was the typical evening in the Daniels household—his father quiet, almost in his own world while Matt and his mom tried to keep the conversation going around them. Now, he'd headed into the living room to watch a game or something while they cleaned up.

"Rested, I guess," Matt replied though he didn't feel he looked any different than he had before. For a while, he'd felt better but now it was as if his insides were twisting up again, only in other ways. Ways that included Ollie. Ways that made him scared of where they were heading...or what they had done...because he didn't know where to go from here. Because the mixed-up thoughts he'd had in his head regarding his friend scared him.

"There you go, shutting down. I hear it in the change of your voice. You and your dad are more alike than either of you realize."

Matt huffed at that one because he and his father were nothing alike. They had never been no matter how many times Matt had wished he could be more like him when he was a child and no matter how much he knew his father wished Matt was more like him too.

"How's Oliver doing?" she asked. Of course, she would switch the subject to something else he didn't want to talk about.

"He's Ollie. He'll always be doing well." And he would too. Oliver didn't realize it but he was the strongest person Matt knew. There wasn't a doubt in his mind Oliver would be exactly where he was, even if he hadn't had the head starts his family had given him. Doing well and doing the right thing were engraved into his bones, sewn into every stitch that held him together.

"His writing is going well?" she asked as Matt rinsed a plate she'd handed him and put it in the rack. They had a dishwasher now, but he doubted they used it very much.

"Seems to be." He wondered then if anyone else knew about Oliver's secret pen name. If his parents knew or if Chance and

Miles knew.

"Okay, what's going on? You're never this quiet when it comes to Oliver," she told him as she washed another dish, before handing that to him as well.

Obviously, his mother was out for blood tonight. "I don't know what you want me to say, Ma. He's writing. He's happy. He's doing what he was meant to do the way we always knew he would. He's still funny and caring and loyal as a man can be. He's…" Matt shrugged. "He's Ollie. He's special. He always will be."

The dish in his mother's hand slipped out and splashed into the water beneath. A soft gasp pushed past her lips and Matt turned toward her to see what had happened.

Her lips made a soft "O" before her chin began to quiver gently. "Oh, Matty."

He heard the knowledge she thought she knew in those two simple words. Heard the surprise there, with a hint of sadness she likely didn't know teased the edges.

"It's nothing, Ma."

"No…it's something. And honestly, I don't know how I never saw it before. Maybe when you were teenagers, I wondered. Viv had said something was going on, but then you went off to New York, and the thought never entered my mind again. You're in love with him, aren't you?"

The truth had always been there, a seed Matt refused to plant or let get any sunlight. He kept it hidden in the deepest, darkest places inside of him. It didn't matter if Oliver had feelings for him too because there was a part of Matt that would never feel good enough for him. Pretty wasn't pretty forever. Shine faded, and beneath was a dullness that Matt didn't know how to see past. He didn't know what he had to offer someone like Oliver. So, he told his mom what he'd been telling himself since he was young, "No, Ma, I'm not in love with him."

"It…it would be okay if you were. You know that, right? You know that your father and I love you and support you. We want nothing more than for you to be happy."

The thing was, Matt didn't know how to be happy. He knew how to fake it. He got close enough to touch the edges of happiness at times—the symphony, spending time with Ollie, the euphoria he felt when he first moved to New York and was determined to make his dreams come true, but real happiness had yet to penetrate his walls.

At the same time, he also knew what his mother told him was true. They did love him and accept him and want him to be happy. But that didn't mean it wouldn't make the divide between them even larger. "I know…but can you imagine how much more awkward this night would have been if Oliver had been here with me as my boyfriend? It's bad enough that he doesn't know how to talk to me but—"

"Is that what you think, Matthew?"

"That's what I know," he replied. "And it's what you know too."

"Your father isn't good at talking to anyone. He's not even the best at talking with me. That doesn't mean he doesn't love us."

Again, Matt knew that was true, but it didn't change the fact that he needed his father to be able to speak with him. He needed to hear his father tell him he loved him.

CHAPTER TWENTY-THREE

IT WAS THE night before Matt's photo shoot. He told Oliver they had to be there at five the next morning because he had to go in for hair and makeup beforehand. It was strange hearing Matt talk about those things, those typical parts of his life and career—the same way edits and plotting were a part of Oliver's days.

The difference was, Matt spoke about it with dread in his voice, like he was on trial, the jury had finished negotiating, and he knew the odds were against him.

He was nervous, he had been all day. If Oliver was being honest, he'd admit that Matt had acted differently since they had sex Friday night, but could he really blame him? A lot had gone down between them that night, things that needed to be said but things that also profoundly affected their friendship.

Going to his parents' house hadn't helped though Oliver knew it wouldn't.

He looked over at his friend who sat at the other end of the couch, flipping through the channels of the television neither of them was really watching.

"Come on," Oliver told him before he stood and held out his hand.

"I don't really feel like going anywhere. Plus, we have to be up early in the morning."

"We're not leaving the house, I promise. Come with me, Matty." Oliver didn't drop his arm, just continued to stand there waiting for Matt to take his hand. He would. Oliver knew that. He had to because no matter what had happened, no matter how different their feelings for each other were, he knew Matt trusted him. Matt likely trusted him more than he did anyone else.

It was a moment later that Matt took his hand. It was cold to the touch, smaller than his own.

He led Matt to the kitchen first, where Oliver let go of him long enough to pull a box of Lucky Charms from the cabinet.

"I'm not hungry," Matt told him but Oliver just ignored him.

He went for the stairs next and despite Matt's groan, he followed behind Ollie. On the way, he opened the hall closet, pulled out a blanket and two battery-operated lanterns.

"What? Are we going camping in your bedroom?" Matt asked.

"No, asshole. Now stop trying to be a prick, and be patient." Their eyes latched on to each other before Matt gave him a small nod in what Oliver hoped was solidarity.

This was ridiculous in a way. Juvenile in a hundred other ways but he hoped it would help.

Oliver went to the far end of the hallway on his second floor. He opened the spare room door, turned on the light and stepped inside.

Matt didn't argue with him, didn't ask what Oliver was doing as he walked over to the large window and unlatched it. It swung ajar, the only window in his house that opened that way.

Oliver turned on the lanterns, handed one to Matt before he stepped onto the stool beneath the window and climbed out. When he got to the roof, he turned to look at Matt and saw the realization in his eyes. "You remember that?" Matt asked, his voice soft and full of wonder.

"I'm only twenty-eight, Matty. I'm not losing my memory yet."

Matt's house had been small growing up and didn't leave much privacy. He had his own room of course, but it was so cluttered he used to say he never felt like he had his own space. When he'd wanted to be alone, he used to pull a ladder out of the shed in the backyard, lean it against the house, and climb onto the roof. He couldn't do it much during the day because the damn thing would be too hot, but at night, the roof had always been Matt's place. There were a few times Oliver had gone up there with him too.

"Are you coming or not?" Oliver asked.

A pause, and then, "I'm coming," whispered past Matt's lips. He climbed out of the window and onto the roof. Off to the right, the roof lowered, flattened so it wasn't at a sharp angle, a benefit Oliver hadn't planned but the design of the house had given him.

He set the box of cereal down, laid the blanket out, before sitting down on top of it. Matt paused again, watching Oliver with those expressive fucking eyes that tied Oliver in knots. They said more than Matt's mouth ever would. Maybe more than his mind or his heart would let him see.

"I forgot what it's like to have someone do things like this for me," Matt said before he sat down beside Oliver. "I'm not sure I deserve it, but thank you."

The moon hung low and full in the sky, adding to the light the lanterns provided them. "Of course you deserve it. It's not different from you knowing I needed to go to the museum that day. Those are the kinds of things people do for one another when they love them—Miles and Chance would do the same thing. That's what friends do." He'd put himself out there, they'd had their talk and each of them knew where they stood. Oliver wouldn't make this about anything more than friendship because that was what they had, and he would be okay with that.

"Okay," Matt replied, but he didn't sound as though he believed Oliver.

Oliver opened the box of cereal, stuck his hand in and grabbed a handful before passing the box to Matt. He didn't take it at first, and the worry in Oliver's gut multiplied. "Take the fucking box, Matty," he told him. Matt chuckled, and stuck his hand into the box he let Oliver continue to hold and pulled out a handful of his own.

They sat on the roof and ate the whole fucking box of Lucky Charms. They spoke some, were quiet for long stretches too. When they finished eating, Oliver set the box beside him and then lay on his back, just a few seconds before Matt did the same.

"It's beautiful out here, Ollie," Matt said from beside him.

"Are you doing okay? I know you're nervous about tomorrow." What Oliver didn't understand exactly, was why.

"I will be. I'm always okay. I just…I know it sounds crazy but I don't like all those eyes on me. It makes me feel like I'm naked." Oliver looked over at Matt just as Matt shook his head. "It makes me feel more than naked—naked I could deal with. It makes…it makes me feel like a fraud."

Oliver's pulse jackhammered. He opened his mouth to tell Matt he wasn't a fraud, but Matt began speaking again before he could. "I get sick sometimes beforehand. I get sick sometimes during breaks. I'll go to the bathroom, vomit, then clean up and pretend everything is okay."

"Jesus, Matty. And Parker never stopped you?"

He rolled his head until he was looking at Oliver. "Parker never knew."

The motherfucker must have been a shitty boyfriend and agent. How could he not see that Matt had been hurting? They'd lived together for years, worked together for even longer. How could he not have known?

"Why do you do it? Christ, Matt. Why do you do that to yourself?" Oliver rolled to his side. He couldn't stop himself from reaching out and pushing Matt's brown hair off his forehead, from twisting a lock of it around his finger.

"It's all I can do—"

"Fuck that."

"I didn't tell you that to argue with you. I told you because I needed to get it out. Because you're the only person in the fucking world I can tell some things to. I just needed you to hear it, not try and fix it for me or not try to tell me what I can or can't do. What I should or shouldn't do. I just needed you to hear it."

Which felt like taking a hammer to his own heart, for Oliver. It felt like letting someone he loved suffer and nothing ate away at him like that did. "Okay." He pulled his hand away and listened. Listened as Matt told him that he sometimes had what sounded a lot like stage fright or anxiety to him. As he told him, he would sometimes go into another room, nearly lose his mind, and then steady himself before he walked back out to pretend nothing was wrong.

"I'm afraid of gaining weight. I know you think I have an eating disorder but I don't…I could, though. If you hadn't been here, I wouldn't have touched that box of cereal because if I gain weight I won't get jobs, but at the same time, every fucking time I take on another one, every contract I sign, I feel like I'm selling my goddamned soul to the devil because I hate it, Ollie. I hate it so fucking much I can't breathe sometimes."

Oliver listened as Matt got it all off his chest, as he opened up to Oliver, even though every word made the rage and pain inside him spin faster and with more strength until he nearly couldn't hold back the storm inside of him.

Matt had been suffering all these years, and he hadn't known. None of them had known. Matt had hidden it from them. Parker hadn't seen the signs, but he should have known. *Not Parker. Fuck Parker.* Somehow, Oliver should have known.

When Matt was done speaking, he moved closer to Oliver. Grabbed Oliver's arm and put it around him and let his head rest on Oliver's shoulder. "Look at the stars with me before we go inside."

Every fucking thing inside of him wanted to tell Matt he shouldn't go tomorrow. That he should be done with modeling but he didn't. He tried to honor Matt's wishes because he knew that Matt felt like this was all he had.

He ran his hand up and down Matt's arm as Matt wrapped around him. He wasn't sure how long it was they lay on his roof, breathing and looking at the stars.

Eventually, they packed up their stuff and went back inside. Matt followed Oliver to his room; Oliver didn't mention it and when Matt stripped down to his blue briefs and climbed into Oliver's bed, he went in beside him and held him the rest of the night.

CHAPTER TWENTY-FOUR

FOR SOME REASON, Matt loved being awake early. It felt like the whole world was still asleep, the edge of waking up just about to descend upon them.

He and Oliver got ready in near silence. Nerves ate away at him, gnawing at his bones and making him feel weak. Not just because of the shoot but because of the things he'd admitted to Oliver last night. Things he'd never expected to tell another human being. When the words did emerge, of course it would be Ollie that he spoke them to. There was never a chance of it being anyone else.

"You about ready?" Oliver asked as he peeked his head into Matt's room—no, the spare room at Ollie's house that Matt used.

"Yeah. Let's go."

That was it for their conversation. It was quiet as they walked to Oliver's car. Quiet as Oliver drove to the address Matt had given him. Quiet as Matt ignored his vibrating phone because he knew it would be Parker, and he didn't feel like talking to the man right now.

Parker wasn't a bad man—he wasn't. Matt knew he cared for him, but then how much could he care when Matt had never fully let him in?

When they pulled up to the mansion where Matt's shoot was, he had to hand his ID to a guard at the gate so they would let him in. Once they were buzzed through, Oliver found a place to park.

He would speak now, Matt knew it so he got out of the car

before Oliver had the chance. That didn't stop his friend, though—it never would. He hurried out and grabbed Matt by the arm as he tried to walk away.

"You wanna walk away; we get in the car right now and leave," he said. Matt couldn't help but smile at the honorable, yet naïve sentiment.

"It's my job, remember? And you sound like I'm going to war or something. I've done this a thousand times. I'll freak out on the inside, hide it on the outside, and get through it. It's not a big deal."

Oliver's eyes turned down, sadness bleeding out of his features. "Anything that hurts you or scares you or makes you uncomfortable is a big deal, Matty. When are you going to realize that?"

Jesus, this man was incredible. Did anyone love the way Oliver did? "You're all heart, Ollie. I've always loved and admired that about you. It's fine. I'm fine."

Ollie sighed but then he leaned forward, cupped the side of Matt's head, fingers in his hair and kissed Matt's forehead.

"Time to forge into battle, sir?" Matt asked, trying to release the pent-up tension inside of him and around them as well.

"I got your back, Matty. Always."

Yeah…yeah, he knew Oliver did. "Come on. Let's get this over with."

As soon as they got inside, Matt was ushered away. He made sure they settled Oliver in with coffee in a lounge area and then it was makeup and wardrobe.

He wasn't the cover boy for the brand, so he wasn't the only model here. Everyone was laughing and joking and directing orders, talking about clothing, and someone who fucked up the lighting. Each word was a distant buzz in Matt's ear. He'd perfected the art of toning people down, of partially tuning them out enough that they didn't feel like a megaphone in his brain.

He felt the familiar rise of the tide in his gut but he rode the waves well, steadying himself to find a way to calm the seas.

"Matt, they'll be ready for you in five," a young man with blue hair and gorgeous makeup told him.

"Thanks. Can you make sure my friend Oliver is there? Get him settled into the back of the room. They know he's watching. Parker called and arranged it."

The assistant nodded and exited the room.

Matt bent over, took steadying, deep breaths. He hated this. Jesus, he fucking hated it. Hated the flash of cameras and the eyes on him. Hated that the only reason he was worthy of being here was because of superficial shit. Hated the feeling of being laid bare, where people could see him. When it wasn't really who he was because music was the only place he was truly himself.

And then...then he stood up. He turned off his emotions, steeled himself because that was what he did. Went on autopilot, got the job done and walked away. He'd become a robot to it, thankful at least for that.

When he walked out of the room, he wasn't the Matt who'd grown up with Oliver. He wasn't the boy who sat on his roof or went to the museum with his friend. He wasn't the guy who ate Lucky Charms until he got nauseous or the man whose soul was made of music.

He was the man he'd made himself into. The one who survived. The one who went to New York and made something of himself even if it wasn't what he'd planned. He was the fighter. The man who fit in. Who didn't feel like an outsider in his family, or an outsider with his friends...all his friends except Oliver, at least. He was the person who took charge of his own life, the way he needed to do.

He walked out of the room wearing the façade that now fit so well, the mask he needed.

When he stepped into the room, his eyes immediately sought

out Oliver. He was there, hands in his pockets, toward the back of the room, all strength and support, his eyes ensnaring Matt, worry embedded deeply in the set of his body.

Matt gave him a small smile to say he was okay because he was. He made sure he was always okay.

———⁓———

OLIVER HAD A whole new appreciation for what Matt did. There was shot after shot, discussion after discussion. Frustration and pose and pose and direction and changes of clothes.

They were there until nearly ten that night.

The whole time he looked for it, looked for signs Matt was coming apart at the seams, looked for signs that he felt like he would burst out of his own body, but Oliver never saw them.

He never fucking saw one…and as much as he wanted to believe it was because Matt didn't feel them, as much as he was angry at himself because he felt like he knew Matt better than anyone in the world, and if anyone could see them it should be him, it only made him realize how good Matt was at pretending. At running the course. At burying the way he felt and moving forward. And that? That broke his heart.

He hated the fact that Matt was so good at feigning everything was okay. How often did he wear that mask? How long had he been hurting and no one had seen it?

"We're going to stop and get you something to eat," Oliver told him as they made their way through LA.

"Okay," Matt replied and he was thankful the other man hadn't argued.

They stopped at a drive-through sandwich place Oliver liked that was open late, and they both ate in the car while Oliver drove them back out to Laurel Canyon.

"That was an intense day," Oliver told him as they pulled into his driveway, the motion light coming on as they did. "I didn't know it was so…intense," he said again because he wasn't sure what other word to use for it.

"Yeah, it is. It wasn't what I expected either, at first. I'm fucking beat but I know there's not a chance in hell I could go to sleep yet." Matt got out of the car, and Oliver did the same.

"You can take a bath and relax. My en suite has a Jacuzzi tub. You're welcome to use it." It was a ridiculous thing to say because obviously, Matt knew about the tub. Oliver led the way up to the porch, where he unlocked the door and then stepped inside, turning off the alarm.

"Okay," Matt replied. "Come with me."

Oliver's head spun. He'd always prided himself on being a smart man. In his head, he knew he needed to put an end to this because he would just get hurt. He was already getting in too deep with Matt as it was but the romantic in him? That boy at eighteen who wanted to tell Matt that he loved him because he believed they were meant to be, that part of him wanted to believe that maybe they had a chance. That Matt's feelings were evolving. Or maybe they'd always been there and he was accepting them. And the horny part of him? That was the part that just wanted to be naked together with Matt again.

"It's not like I'm turning down that offer." The words felt disingenuous because he used them to make it sound as though this was about sex. Like maybe he'd put on the same kind of mask Matt wore while modeling to say them.

They made their way up the stairs and to Oliver's room. They went straight into the bathroom. It felt like déjà vu, took Oliver back to their shower together that last time he had the chance to be inside of Matt.

He started the water while Matt undressed. He turned Matt's way right as he stripped the last bit of clothing from his body.

Oliver wanted to tell him how fucking beautiful he was, but it was important to him that Matt didn't think that was all Oliver saw when he looked at him.

So he kept his mouth shut and began taking off his own clothes. Matt slipped around him and stepped into the tub. He shut off the water just as Oliver turned and saw that he sat in the middle of it. He put his foot into the warm water—he'd always loved hot baths—and sat behind Matt, one leg on either side of him. Matt automatically leaned back against Oliver's chest.

Oliver ran his hand up and down Matt's slender torso, let his fingers play along his hip bones. "I would never have known," he said.

Somehow, Matt knew exactly what he meant. "That's the point. I've become good at camouflage."

"I should have known. I should have seen it. I—"

"Stop trying to be a hero, Ollie. You can't always be the hero." Matt sighed but then put his hand on Oliver's leg.

"Are you going to keep doing it?" Oliver asked him only to feel Matt tense up slightly.

"I don't want to talk about that but since it's my job, I would say I don't have a choice. How's the book coming?" he asked, and Oliver told him. He'd written like crazy recently so he filled Matt in on all the antics his characters were up to.

They talked and laughed about everything and anything as the water began to get cold. This had always been what Oliver wanted with Matt. The everyday intimacy of a relationship but then, that wasn't what they had here. It was what Matt just said—camouflage.

"I'm exhausted," Matt finally told him. "I think I need to hit the sack. Thank you...for today. You might not know it, but you being there made today a whole lot easier."

Those words were meant to soothe but all they did was grind up Oliver's heart. If he meant so goddamned much to Matt, why were they playing this game? Why couldn't they make it something real?

"That's what I'm here for," Oliver told him, trying to tamp down the bitterness in his voice.

Matt didn't seem to notice. He got out of the bath, grabbed a towel from the rack, wrapped it around himself and then grabbed another for Oliver.

"Are you staying in there all night?" Matt asked, and Oliver felt like he had another mask in place. As though he was going to pretend today hadn't bothered him.

Oliver let the water out, stood and took the towel. He dried himself off before grabbing a pair of underwear from his drawer. He watched Matt, curious what he would do.

Once dry he put the towel into the hamper and then walked over to Oliver's bed and climbed inside.

A slow burn started in Ollie's gut—part want and part bitterness that he didn't understand. He tried to push those feelings aside, ignore them. To live in the moment. That was what he'd told himself he was doing all along with Matt, but the anger was there, building in a way he probably should have known would happen. Why couldn't Matt see what they could be together, what maybe they already were?

CHAPTER TWENTY-FIVE

MATT COULDN'T SLEEP.

There had been a gentle difference, a switch in Oliver tonight that played heavily on his mind.

He doubted he would have been able to rest even if it hadn't been for that because he'd felt the shift inside of himself as well. The evolution of what they were, and that scared him to death.

He didn't have to be in this bed right now.

And even if he was, it didn't have to mean something big…something real but then when it came to himself and Oliver, had he really ever expected something different? Had just a light, hookup ever been a possibility between them?

He'd known that even when he was a teenager, which was the exact reason he'd never let himself touch Oliver, and now it was too late.

Matt slowly eased out of the bed. He looked down, and Oliver didn't move. His breathing was even and steady as he slept.

They'd gone to bed with the bathroom door cracked and the light on. The faint glow allowed him to see Oliver's soft features. People said that about Matt, but there was a hardness in him Ollie could never have. He hadn't lived a particularly hard life. He knew that. There hadn't been any major traumas that happened to him, yet he didn't know how to see the world the way Oliver did. Didn't know how to love it…didn't know how to love himself.

Matt turned and slipped out of the room, closing the door quietly behind him. He made a quick stop to the spare bedroom where he pulled on a pair of sweats that hung low on his slender hips before padding his way down Oliver's stairs.

He needed to play.

Music and Oliver had always been the only two things that centered him.

Matt made his way to the piano, the one he'd played all those years ago in Oliver's house. He turned on the floor lamp that stood beside it before he pulled out the bench and sat down.

It was automatic, the calm that started to come over him as his fingers danced across the keys he loved so much. They became an extension of him, of his hand as he gave in to the emotion inside him he released when he played.

He played for the young boy he used to be who wanted nothing more than this, and who'd tried to force himself to believe he could have it.

He played for Oliver who had always had more faith in him than he had in himself.

He played for his parents who did their best to give him music, even when they couldn't afford it, even when they looked at him and saw no traces of themselves.

He played until his heart bled through his fingers. Until his eyes clouded with unshed tears.

He played for the man he was now, who felt like the biggest fraud on Earth. Who smiled for the cameras when he hated what they showed him.

Himself.

He knew Oliver was watching him before he moved closer, knew he was there before he spoke. Slowed his fingers on the keys just as his friend said, "There you are."

"You knew where I was," he replied, and then, "sorry if I woke you."

"That's not what I meant. Earlier, during your shoot you had your walls so fucking high around you, I couldn't see *you*. I looked for you, even afterward but you had your mask firmly in place. You do most of the time, don't you, Matty? You're always fucking wearing it but not when you play. That's the only time you're really you."

"I'm not sure if I'm even me then," he answered honestly because how could it truly be who he was if he didn't believe in it? As real as it felt, it also seemed like it was distanced from him, not attached.

He turned around on the bench, wrapped his arms around Oliver's waist and pulled him closer. Rubbed his face against Oliver's abs, feeling the hairs of the trail that led down to his underwear against his cheek.

Oliver's hands went into his hair, his fingers knotted in it, as he held Matt close.

All he could think about in that moment was how much he needed Oliver. He shouldn't, but that was the truth of them. He'd always needed Oliver.

Matt kissed his stomach, brushed his lips in a path toward the edge of his underwear.

"Matty…" Oliver's voice was rough…greedy…hungry, but Matt also knew what he would say next. Knew he would try to talk and he couldn't talk right now.

"Please. Christ, I want you so fucking much." When he heard the low growl that started in Oliver's gut push past his lips, Matt slid his hands into the back of Oliver's underwear. He eased them down and wrapped his mouth around the head of Oliver's swollen erection the second it burst free.

He was already leaking and Matt lapped at the pre-come before sucking him again. Oliver's hand in his hair tightened, giving him a sharp sting that just ratcheted him up even more.

"Jesus, Matty, you make me so fucking wild. Like I could live off nothing but you."

Matt kissed his way down to Oliver's sac, sucked one of his heavy balls into his mouth, loving the feel of the rough hair there against his face. "Me too," he admitted. "Christ, me too."

Oliver jerked him to his feet. With rough, greedy hands he pulled at Matt's sweats. Loving every second of it, of this demanding, starving Oliver, he wanted nothing more than him.

Matt took over for Oliver, pulling off his own sweats as Oliver made work of his underwear. Then the other man was pushing the bench out of the way, backing Matt up against the piano until his ass hit the keys.

"I've always wanted to take you right here on this piano. I used to jerk off thinking about it every fucking day, bending you over it and owning your ass."

"Oh, fuck." Matt's cock twitched against his stomach, liking the idea of that very fucking much.

Oliver lifted him, set him down on the keys. His mouth came down hard on Matt's just as Matt wrapped his legs around Oliver's waist.

The kiss was filled with years of want, years of need, years of denial.

Each time they moved, another sound came out of the piano—rough, random notes.

Oliver thrust against him, rubbing their erections together as he continued to devour Matt's mouth.

It wasn't long before he licked a trail down Matt's neck, sucked the skin of his throat as Matt arched toward him.

His balls felt like they were on fire with the need to let loose.

"Fuck me, Ollie. Please. I need your cock in my ass so bad I can't breathe."

Oliver pulled away, reached for something and then stopped, as though he forgot where they were. "Shit. I need a condom. Don't move. I want you right here when I get back."

He tried to walk away but Matt grabbed ahold of him. "I've never gone raw with anyone…" There was a brilliant explosion of desire in Oliver's eyes before Matt continued. "Not even Parker. Because we played we always used condoms with each other and with anyone else. I get checked regularly too."

The brightness in his eyes dimmed then, "It's okay if you don't want to. Go get one. I shouldn't have said anything."

"Shut up, Matty. Just shut up. Don't fool yourself into believing I don't want to be raw inside of you. I've never done that either, and I've been checked too. I just hate the fact that he had you…all those fucking years he had you, and he shared you. If you were mine, I'd burn the fucking world down before I let anyone else touch you."

He knew Oliver well enough to realize he didn't mean any offense. He wasn't the type to look down on anyone else or their decisions, but he wasn't built to be able to share someone he cared about. Not everyone was. In that moment, Matt thought that if Oliver were his, he would feel the same way.

Matt eased off the piano. They stood naked, chest-to-chest, right in front of it. Matt pushed up and pressed his lips to Oliver's, teased them open with his mouth.

When Oliver's arms wrapped around him, it was a confirmation for both of them.

Matt reached over and picked up the bottle of lotion he'd moved by the piano because he had dry hands.

He handed it to Oliver, who squirted some in his hand. Raw hunger radiated off him, making Matt come undone.

Matt turned around, leaned over the piano with his ass out. He groaned when Oliver palmed his cheeks before spreading them. "Jesus, that fucking hole, Matty. I'd bury my cock in it every fucking day of my life if you'd let me." He rubbed his lotion-slicked fingers down Matt's crack before tapping on his asshole. "Finger it, lick it, make love to it. I just want to be inside you any way I can."

You are, Matt wanted to tell him but couldn't make the words leave that dark place he kept them hidden.

He let out a deep breath when Oliver pushed his first finger past his ring of muscles and inside of him.

Oliver leaned over him, kissed the back of his neck and his shoulder as he fingered Matt's hole.

"You feel so good inside. How am I going to handle having my dick inside you with nothing between us? You go straight to my head. To my heart."

Matt pushed his ass back, needing more. Oliver knew exactly what he wanted, pushing another lotioned finger inside of him.

He worked Matt open, rubbing his fingers across his prostate. Each time he did, a sharp breath ripped from his lungs.

"Hurry. Get your fucking dick inside of me. Please," Matt pleaded.

When Oliver's fingers pulled out of him, he almost begged for Ollie to just hurry and put them back in. He needed something, any part of Ollie, inside of him.

Oliver didn't leave him waiting long. He pumped more lotion into his hand, stroked his cock and then the swollen head was there, stretching Matt open and pushing inside.

He fought to clutch onto the piano but could only grip the left side as Ollie slowly, so fucking slowly, breached him.

"Oh, fuck if feels so good inside of you. God, there's nothing like it." He pushed in deeper. "I can't even find the words, Matty. You're melting my fucking brain."

The second he was buried to the hilt, stretching him and savoring that full feeling that Matt loved so fucking much, Oliver pulled almost all the way out, before railing into him again.

"Christ, Ollie. So good. So fucking good." Matt's cock leaked on the piano, his balls tighter and tighter with each slow thrust of Oliver's hips.

He wrapped one arm around Matt's waist, used the other hand to reach out and stroke Matt's aching erection.

He made love to Matt slowly—that was what he was doing, he realized. Oliver was making love to him, maybe he always had been and Matt had been too fucking chickenshit to admit it.

Every so often, one of them would hit a key on the piano. Oliver leaned over him, kissed his shoulder as he pumped his dick in and out of Matt's ass.

He wanted Oliver's come inside him, wanted to feel each hot spurt coating him. Every time he thrust, he hit Matt's prostate. He stroked Matt's cock faster, kissed his shoulder and whispered, "I am so goddamned lost inside you."

When Oliver's teeth nipped his shoulder, Matt couldn't hold back anymore. Hot come spurted from his slit, and when Oliver stroked him again, he let loose again, his orgasm rocking through him so hard his knees went weak, making him collapse against the piano.

"Oh, fuck. Oh God, Matt. I…" And then Oliver's cock jerked. He felt the warm gush of Oliver's come paint his insides, making his cock slide more easily in and out of Matt's hole. "Fuck," Oliver gritted out a second time, shoved himself deep, his dick spasming again as he rode out the final waves of his orgasm.

And he didn't want it to end.…Matt didn't fucking want it to stop and he didn't know how to handle that.

CHAPTER TWENTY-SIX

H E'D NEVER COME so hard in his life. His heart felt like it swelled too big to fit in his chest. He'd always known he loved Matt. Everyone had always known it but in that moment, he wondered how he'd ever breathed without him.

Miles and Chance would laugh that off, call him a hopeless romantic with stars in his eyes but here? Right now? It didn't fucking matter.

He pulled out, his dick beginning to soften. They were sweaty, come and lotion all over but he didn't give a shit. Oliver picked Matt up and carried him to the couch, where he lay down with him.

Matt's arms went around him. He nuzzled into Matt's neck and breathed him in. "You turn me inside out. I don't want to ever stop touching you," he said into Matt's throat.

There was a pause, and then Matt's soft voice. "I know....This is going to be harder to stop than I realized. I…"

Oliver froze up. "Why do we have to stop, Matt? Seriously. Give me one fucking reason why we have to stop."

"Because I live in New York and you live in LA, is a good one."

Oliver rolled his eyes. "So? I'd give it a shot. It's not like it would be difficult for me to travel. Fuck, I could *move* there if we wanted. I can work from anywhere."

Matt jerked up into a sitting position. "Move to New York? Where did that come from? Your family is here."

Oliver tried not to roll his eyes. "Chill out. I'm not talking about moving there tomorrow, if ever. I'm just saying that's a bullshit excuse and you know it. Fuck, you could move here just as easily if you wanted to."

He sat too, his leg bouncing up and down. He probably shouldn't have started this, not right now but Jesus, he was so fucking tired of pretending. Of the excuses. In or out. They needed to make a decision now. Matt couldn't keep running.

"My life is in New York. I don't want to move back here."

"A life you fucking hate!" Oliver bellowed, a sudden anger bursting through him. Everything out of Matt's mouth was an excuse. Oliver loved him, *fucking loved him*, and Matt just wanted to throw that away? Over a job he hated and a bullshit excuse? Couldn't he just want to try? Especially when there was a part of him that had started to believe Matt might love him too.

"You said you knew what this was, Ollie. You said you wouldn't ask for more. Christ, now you're talking about moving?" Matt shoved to his feet in a move that didn't surprise Oliver.

He shook his head. "And you know you're in love with me too, but you're too fucking scared to admit it! All this is just nothing but an excuse, an excuse for you to admit you might give a shit about something, including yourself! Stay in New York. Move to Los Angeles. Who gives a shit what you do, but quit your fucking job. You know I'd help you if you need it. Fuck, maybe I can ask around and see if I can help you get things on track with your music."

Matt's eyes threw daggers at him, angry lasers that shot straight through Oliver's chest. "You can never fucking stop it, can you? Stop trying to save me, Ollie." He ran a rough hand through his hair. "I don't need you to save me!"

Oliver couldn't help but push to his feet at that. Anger caught fire in his chest, devastating everything in its wake as it ripped through him. "Then stop fucking acting like it! Jesus, look at yourself, Matty! You say you can take care of yourself, that you don't need me, then what the fuck are you doing? You came here, to me, when shit fell apart. You gave up on your music years ago. You continue to do a job you hate and don't even try for anything else. You're too damn skinny because you don't even fucking eat well, but you don't need me to take care of you? Fucking prove it. Grow up and do something. Stop making excuses and fight."

The devastation on Matt's face nearly stole his breath. The second he'd spit those words out, he wanted them back. Wished like hell they had never formed in his brain.

Matt stood rigidly, his body like it was made of stone, pain bleeding from his features, from the fresh wound Oliver had given him. "Shit…I didn't mean to say that. I—" Oliver tried to take a step toward him, but Matt shook his head.

"Fuck you, Ollie. You've made it perfectly clear how you feel. Now you finally see what I've always known. I'm not good enough for the perfect Oliver Hayes. The guy who always has the answers and always does the right thing. You would never have a relationship like I've had, and you would never give up on a dream but then, you wouldn't have to. You've never known what it's like not to get what you want."

That wasn't true because Oliver didn't have him. He opened his mouth to say something, what he didn't know, but Matt beat him to it. "Don't. There's nothing to say. I'll be out of your hair within an hour."

"Of course you will," Oliver said honestly. He hated the truth that he had to admit but if he didn't, he would never get past this. He would never get over Matt. He saw now more than ever, that he needed to. "You always run the second something gets tough. It's what you do best."

Matt stared at him, grinding his teeth so hard Oliver could see his jaw lock. Then, without a word, he turned and went for the stairs.

CHAPTER TWENTY-SEVEN

O LIVER RAN HIS finger along the edge of his glass. It was Friday night. Miles and Chance sat beside him at their table. People danced, lights flashed, music pumped through the speakers as it did every Friday night, but it felt muted to him. Like his pulse didn't beat with the life around him the way it usually did. He didn't like it. That the completeness he always felt spending time with the two men beside him just wasn't there. He was always at ease with his friends but tonight? Tonight he just felt like shit.

It had been a few days since Matt left. Oliver assumed he was back in New York but considering they hadn't spoken to each other, he didn't know. Every time Matt had left Los Angeles in the past, he'd always let Oliver know when he was safe in New York. Maybe that was silly but it was one of those things that had never changed through the years.

Oliver glanced at Chance, who bobbed his head to the music. Next, he turned his head toward Miles, who was busy watching a go-go dancer a few feet away from them.

Oliver hadn't said anything to Miles and Chance about his fight with Matt or the fact that Matt left. There wasn't a doubt in his mind that they wondered where Matt was and they would mention it. He would give them until five…four…three…two…

"What's wrong, baby boy?" Chance nudged him softly in his side, and Oliver chuckled. He'd known it and despite how he felt, he found some comfort in that. In his friends and their relationship.

"What's so funny?" Chance asked.

"Nothing. I just know you guys well."

Miles sighed beside him. "And we know you well. Let me guess, Matt left? Likely at the last minute?"

Oliver dropped his head against the back of the bench seat. He didn't have a choice. They'd have this out. There wasn't a chance they'd let this slide and the truth was, he would be just as determined as them if the situation was reversed so he decided he should just get it over with now. "Yes, he did." He looked Chance's way. "We were fucking, by the way."

"What?" Chance lurched forward. "Why didn't I know that shit? I'm always the last one to know everything."

"Because you're better at trying to mind your own business than I am," Miles answered and then added, "get up."

"Huh?" Oliver asked even though he'd heard what Miles said. He was staying in this seat. He was fairly safe where he was.

"I said get up," Miles repeated. "Let's go. We're not talking about this here. Let's go to Chance's."

Chance lived in the heart of West Hollywood, not too far from Wild Side. They could walk to his place in less than ten minutes, and it was probably smart. They would do this one way or another and it would be a lot less embarrassing getting scolded at Chance's place than it would at Wild Side.

Dare was behind the bar tonight. He gave them a sexy smirk when they approached him. "You heading out early tonight?" he asked.

"Yeah, our boy got his heart broken," Chance replied.

"Jesus fucking Christ, Chance. Thanks a lot." Oliver's life would be a whole lot easier if he could hate them. He tried really, really hard sometimes.

"He's pretty enough to break any man's heart." Dare winked at him. Apparently, it was pretty fucking obvious he was gone for

Matt.

"Well, any man but me," Dare continued. "Austin has me on lockdown."

Everyone except Oliver chuckled, then Miles took over like he did so well, saying they needed to go. They cleared out their tab with Dare and then headed down Robertson before they hung a left and went to Chance's apartment.

He lived in a small, one bedroom. He could afford much more than what he had but that was the way Chance worked. In some ways, he was more high maintenance than Miles or Oliver, but in others, he was the simplest of them all.

The second they were enclosed inside his place, Oliver walked over and sat on the red couch that he wouldn't let within a mile of his house. Who the hell had a red couch? But it fit Chance perfectly. He was more the typical, quirky artist in ways Oliver and Miles weren't.

"I fucking told you, Ollie. I *told* you to be careful when it comes to Matt. But did you listen? No. And before you rip open your jacket to reveal your hero cape, it's not because Matt's a bad guy; he's just not the right guy for you. I knew this would happen. I fucking knew it." Miles crossed his arms, looking at Oliver as though he was a child instead of a grown-ass man.

"Chill the fuck out, Miles, and cut him some slack. We know how he feels about Matt and he's obviously hurting. The last thing he needs is you going into bossy daddy mode on him. He has the cape; you're the disciplinarian. Fucking hell, why do I hang out with you two? Plus, there's more important shit to discuss. I really want to know what it was like to fuck Matt. I'd be lying if I didn't admit I always wondered what it would be like to have some of that ass." Oliver's eyes went wide and Chance continued, "Not that I would have. Friend code and that shit but he's gorgeous. Probably was a lousy fuck. Most of the extremely pretty boys don't work real hard because they don't feel like they have to."

There was a pause, the room quiet except for the ticking of the clock on Chance's wall before all three men let out loud laughter simultaneously. Oliver's gut cramped, he laughed so hard; tears leaked from his eyes as he replayed Chance's speech in his head. God, he loved these men. As much as he'd been hurting, this helped.

When he had finally settled down enough to speak, he said, "I needed that," which he knew had been the reason Chance had said it. That was what they did for each other, all of them, and they always had. There wasn't a doubt in his mind that they always would, either. They were so fucking lucky, all of them. But that didn't mean he didn't still feel the loneliness creeping through him. As much as he loved them, something was missing. It always was.

The emptiness was back, that vast barren space inside him that had always belonged to Matt.

Oliver sighed. "For a while there, I really fucking thought things could be different with us. That we could work." What he didn't say because he knew they wouldn't believe him, was that he knew, somehow he fucking *knew* Matt loved him too. He saw it in the way Matt looked at him, felt it in the way Matt held him. The way he opened up to Oliver in ways he didn't with anyone else. But Matt had been telling the truth when he said he was too afraid to let himself admit he loved Oliver. It didn't matter what Oliver believed he knew, though. Even if Matt loved him, that just wasn't enough.

Miles came over first and sat on his right, then Chance on his left. Oliver put his hand on Chance's knee and his head on Miles's shoulder and when he did, it made him even more sad, but not for himself, for Matt. Did he have this with anyone? This friendship that Oliver had with Chance and Miles. Yes, he'd had it with Oliver, but did he have it anywhere else? Did he have it in New York with Parker or any of his other friends? Because as much as they'd all hung out, the bond Matt had with Chance and Miles hadn't been as strong as the bond Oliver had with them. He couldn't imagine going through life without them by his side. Without always having people there he could lean on. His heart broke for people who weren't this lucky...or who didn't let themselves be.

"Do you want to talk about it?" Miles asked him.

"No," he answered honestly. Talking about it was the last thing he wanted to do. "I don't much see the point. We fought. He left." The end. It wasn't the ending Oliver would have chosen, but it was the one he received.

"And he should have left, Ollie. He should have," Miles answered making Oliver tense up. "No, hear me out," Miles continued. "I'm not trying to be a dickhead here but...I think it's time to be honest with yourself. You know Matt better than any of us. Maybe you have more answers than we do, but even I know that there's something going on with him. That there's always been something going on with him on the inside." Miles touched his chest. "Where no one can fix it but Matt himself. Not you, me, Chance, his family. No one but Matt. Until he does fix it, there was never a chance between the two of you because you would enable him, baby. You know you would. You're a fixer and a caregiver, and you would have given him every fucking drop of who you are, and it wouldn't have been enough because Matt has to heal Matt. Eventually, it would have eaten away at you, at who *you* are, and *that's* always been my main problem. You would have ended up resenting him and hated yourself for it."

Miles took a deep breath and then continued, "Matt needs to fix Matt, and you need to realize that you can't be his or anyone else's savior. The shit between the two of you—it's not all on him, Ollie. You have to learn to put yourself first. You have to learn that while it's okay to support people, you aren't responsible for their happiness."

Oliver let Miles's words sink in. Let them grow roots inside of him.

Chance put his hand over Oliver's and squeezed. Miles leaned over and kissed his forehead. Both of them offering support.

Oliver's pulse echoed with a loud thump in his ear. His chest got heavy with the weight of the truth Miles had just spoken. The truth he'd likely known but wouldn't admit to himself.

Miles was right. Oliver knew he was right. Maybe part of him had already started to resent Matt, which was why he'd unleashed the other night and said all the things he did.

And Matt…he was lost beyond what Oliver had known before this visit. Until Matt faced those things, he would never be able to fully give himself to anyone. He would never truly be happy.

"Wow…that was some deep shit, Miles. I seriously just had a *come to Jesus moment*," Chance said and as much as Oliver didn't feel it, as much as he felt like his whole universe had just altered, he couldn't help but laugh.

Like always, Chance said exactly what needed to be said to break the tension.

The subject was dropped after that and they all knew it. There was nothing else to say. Oliver knew what he had to do.

From there, Chance turned on one of their favorite episodes of Queer as Folk. They watched it together, Oliver only half into it. You knew shit was serious when his favorite show couldn't help.

Later that night, when he was alone in his house, he lay in bed, his sheets still smelling like Matt because he hadn't washed them. The lights were out, the glow of his phone the only thing illuminating the room.

And he dialed.

He wasn't surprised when Matt didn't answer. He could hold a grudge like no one else, especially when he was hurt. Oliver had hurt Matt much like Matt had hurt Oliver.

The second the voicemail beeped for him to leave his message, he spoke. "Hey, Matty. I just…" Oliver closed his eyes and let out a deep breath. "I just called to tell you good-bye. It's about time I did that, huh? I'm not telling you good-bye when it comes to our friendship, but you know that. I'll always be your friend, but that other shit? Loving you and wanting you and waiting for you…I have to let that go. I have to move on. It's better for me…and better for you too. You're right. I would have always tried to be your savior, your hero but the truth is, you have to be your own hero. You'll get there. I know you will. Take care of yourself." And then he hung up and whispered, *"Take care of yourself, Matty,"* before he rolled over and tried like hell to go to sleep.

GOOD-BYE.

Oliver was finally telling him good-bye.

It was likely something he should have done a long time ago but still, even knowing that he couldn't believe the words. No, he knew Oliver was serious. Oliver didn't speak unless he was sure of what he was saying but…how did they come to this?

Matt lay in bed and listened to Oliver's voicemail for the third time before he dropped the phone. The message of course, didn't change…no matter how much he wished it could.

Good-bye.

Take care of yourself.

You'll get there.

Those statements wrestled with things Oliver had said to him during their fight. He knew that nearly every single word Oliver had spoken was true. Matt was fucking up. He'd always been fucking up. He hated his life and everything he stood for—and had for too damn long—yet he didn't do anything about it.

He just kept forging forward and shoving everything else to the side.

Matt looked around the room he'd been sleeping in—the spare room in his and Parker's apartment. The sun beat through the window. It was around noon and he hadn't been out of bed yet. He wore a pair of white underwear and a button-up shirt left open because he'd planned to go out with Parker last night but had changed his mind and then didn't have the will to undress completely.

Ollie had actually told him good-bye, and Matt couldn't blame him for it.

"Get your ass up," Matt mumbled to himself. His mouth was dry, and he needed coffee something fierce.

Matt climbed out of the bed, brushed his teeth and then made his way into the living room.

Parker was at the door, in his underwear, kissing good-bye whomever it was that he'd brought home last night.

As Matt started to make the coffee, Parker closed the door, walked over and said, "You look like shit. Somehow, I have a feeling you didn't look that bad when we broke up. You've always been in love with your LA boy; have you figured that out yet?"

Yes…yes, he had. "I'm not in the mood." He waited for the coffee to brew, inhaling the scent and hoping it helped.

"What are you in the mood for? You haven't left the apartment since you've been back. You reluctantly agreed to go out last night and then canceled at the last moment. I don't think I've seen you eat, and you're sucking down coffee like it's going out of style. I feel like we're in a rom-com."

Matt rolled his eyes, stopped the drip to pour himself a cup and then went over to the kitchen table. "Did you have fun last night?" he asked. It would be much easier to talk about Parker than himself.

"Ah, changing the subject. I didn't see that coming."

Jesus. Now Parker was going to start in on him too? "What do you want from me? I'm in a shitty mood. Do you want me to admit I've always been in love with him? Fine. Yes, I have. That doesn't change anything." They were too different. It would never work. Matt didn't know how to make himself happy. How could he make Oliver happy?

"It should change everything, Matt." There was no hurt in Parker's eyes. No regret that their own relationship had ended. They both knew they'd grown apart a long time ago; maybe they both knew they had never really been in love at all. They'd had fun together and they were friends—there was a difference. "What's holding you back?" Parker asked him.

There was no thought on Matt's part. The answer to that was simple: himself. He was holding himself back.

Stop making excuses and fight.

Grow up.

Good-bye.

Oliver's words started playing games with him again, taunting him and teasing him until he felt like he would lose his mind.

Matt dropped his elbows on the table and let his head rest in his hands. Jesus, this hurt. Losing Ollie would always hurt.

"Do you want to know something?" Parker asked. He didn't wait for Matt to reply before continuing. "I'm not sure I've ever really known you. I wanted to. I know bits and pieces of you, but you've never fully shown me who you are, Matt. Do you realize that? We've been together for years, and I don't know who you are."

Another truth.

Because Matt was afraid to let anyone see who he was….Because he didn't know how to love that person. If he couldn't love himself, how could he expect anyone else to love him? How could he love someone without hurting them?

You'll get there. I know you will.

He wanted to. He really fucking did.

"Who are you, Matt?" Parker asked.

He wasn't sure what made him open his mouth to speak. Maybe it was the fact that Oliver said good-bye but still somehow believed in Matt. There had always been a part of him that wanted to make Oliver proud. "I hate modeling. I always have," Matt admitted. Maybe that wasn't who he was, but it was who he wasn't.

"Oh…well, that's a surprise. I knew you were losing interest, but I didn't realize you'd always hated it. Why do you do it?" Parker asked simply.

The truth slammed into him, a fist to the gut.

Because it wouldn't hurt if he lost it. Not the way it hurt to lose music, to walk away from music. Not the way it hurt to lose Oliver. Nothing could ever hurt like losing and disappointing Oliver. Modeling couldn't crush his heart so it was all he had been able to risk.…

You'll get there. I know you will.

He couldn't risk any more. "I can't keep doing it. I'm done." Just muttering those words felt as if half of the extra weight he carried in his bones melted away. Like he was closer to just being Matt than he'd been before.

"Done. We have no contracts to fulfill so we're good."

Matt's eyes darted up and looked at him. Was it so simple? Maybe it was.

Parker sighed, then asked, "What do you want, Matt? What do you really *want?*"

What did he want? He wanted music. He wanted his family. He wanted Oliver. All those things were encompassed in one thing that he'd run away from for so damn long. "To be happy." He wanted to be happy.

"What are you doing to make that happen?"

Nothing. He'd been doing nothing, for longer than he wanted to admit.

Matt thought about the feeling he had when he played Oliver's piano, when he looked through his old music, when he wrote.

The passion that pumped through his veins when he laughed with Oliver. When they made love. Or talked, or sat on a roof together, or went to the symphony, or to the museum.

He wanted that. He wanted all of it so much he suddenly couldn't breathe.

You'll get there. I know it.

The alternative was to say good-bye, and Matt didn't think he could live with that. He didn't want to.

He wanted *more,* and it was time to do something about it because the pain eating him alive from the inside out? If he didn't stop it now, there would be nothing left of him. There was too much beautiful in the world for that. He'd seen it back home in LA....He even saw it here in his friendship with Parker.

Matt wasn't ready to say good-bye.

Oliver had finally taken that step, finally done what was best for himself...and Matt wanted to do that too. He needed to. "Nothing," he finally answered. "But I think it's time to change that."

CHAPTER TWENTY-EIGHT

Three months later

MATT STOOD IN front of his parents' house. Their car was parked neatly in the driveway. Everything looked exactly as it had a few months ago, yet somehow different at the same time. It was as though he was looking at it through different eyes.

He'd called a week before and let his parents know he would be coming back to Los Angeles because he didn't want to show up out of the blue again. Plus, it would have been hard to keep from them anyway, considering he'd made a deal with his mom that they would speak on the phone at least once a week. It had become their routine the past few months, much like Oliver's routine at Wild Side with Miles and Chance.

He'd never understood why he had kept himself at arm's length with his mom. He and his dad had their issues, but it was different with her. Matt had apologized for that, and it was one of the changes he was making in his life; the distance he'd kept with them was one of his biggest regrets.

Matt closed the door of his new car before making his way up the familiar walkway to the porch. The second his foot hit the bottom step the door jerked open, and his mom stood there.

"I know it's only been a few months, but it's so good to have my boy home again," she said before opening her arms. Matt walked into them and gave her a tight hug. "You feel like you've put on a little weight. Look like it too," she added.

He pulled away and smiled at her. "It feels good to be home, Ma. And I have put on weight. Not a lot but about twelve pounds. I still look good, though." He winked at her, and she waved her hand at him.

"You're so silly. Of course you look good."

Matt followed his mom into the house. His dad rose from the chair slowly as Matt made his way over to him. There was a pause, and then Matt just leaned in, hugging his father with the same strength as he'd just done with his mom. "Hey, Dad. It's good to see you."

"It's good to see you too, son," he replied.

When they parted, the older man moved to sit again. Matt reached out his hand to help him, but his father shook him off. "It's okay, Matthew. I have it."

He sighed, unsure why he expected anything different. Why Matt thought he would suddenly be okay accepting help. Trying not to be frustrated, he moved to sit on the couch beside his father's chair. The three of them sat and talked for a little while about what was going on with Matt, his parents and things like that.

The talk was much like it always was between them, Matt and his mom carrying most of the conversation.

It was about an hour later that Matt's stomach growled. "I'm getting a little hungry for dinner. I'll order us a pizza," he told his mom.

She shook her head. "No, no. I'll take care of it." She made the call, then walked over and grabbed her purse. "I'm going to head over and pick it up."

Matt's eyebrows pulled together. "Why didn't you have it delivered?" It would make things a lot easier. It's what they usually did.

"There's a new pizza place I've been wanting to try—small business. Mom-and-pop place. I figured this would be the perfect time, but they don't deliver."

Matt started to stand. "I'll go with you." It would give them the perfect opportunity to chat some more.

"No." She waved him off. "You had a long flight. Why don't you stay here with your father and relax?"

It was then he realized what she was doing—giving him time with his dad, which they needed. Because sooner or later, they had to hash this out. It was important for both of them. For their relationship. Matt wasn't going to run away from his life or his problems anymore.

He deserved better than that.

"Okay."

She smiled at Matt, kissed his dad good-bye and then left.

"This is a funny part." His dad pointed to the television but Matt didn't look at it. He couldn't.

"I need to talk to you for a second, Dad. Can we turn off the television?" The older man turned and looked at Matt. He had crow's feet around his eyes and a little graying in his hair. When he was younger, he'd always thought his dad could do anything. There was a time when Matt wanted nothing more than to be like him and as he stared at his father, really looked at him—saw the sadness he carried in his bones, he thought maybe they were alike. Maybe both of them had expectations for themselves that never came to fruition, and they both struggled to forgive themselves for it.

Matt had recently learned to forgive himself; it was time his father did too.

"Dad…turn off the television, please," Matt said. He watched as his father picked up the remote and did as Matt asked.

"You know…when I was little, I used to watch you get ready for work every day. You'd come home exhausted, dirty, but you always had a smile on your face. And you always went to work too—even when you were sick. Even when your back would hurt, and Mom would tell you to stay home. You went because it was important to you to do the best damn job you could do, to provide for your family. You never gave up. You never let anything get the best of you. You kept going and all I could think was...that's the kind of man I want to be. I thought one day I'd be heading to the factory to work with you."

Matt looked at his father's hand on the arm of the chair and noticed it was shaking.

"I..." he started. "I didn't know..."

"It's true," Matt told him. "But the older I got, the more I started to realize what I wanted. I fell in love with music and it was like I realized, *yes. This is who I am.* It was like I finally recognized myself. I craved music all the time. At first, it scared me because if I was a composer, I couldn't be you. I looked up to you so damn much, but I thought if I could work half as hard at music—at doing something that I loved—as you'd always worked, then I would be okay. But the more I fell in love with music, the more things that I started to want in my life, the more I felt like I started to disappoint you."

"What?" His father's green eyes went wide. They were the same shade of green as Matt's. "You don't disappoint me, Matthew. How can you think that? Do you know how strong you are? You have always been true to who you are and what you want. Not everyone has the strength to do that. I've never been more proud of anyone than I am of you."

Matt's eyes started to blur, to fill with unshed tears. His father was proud of him? Respected him?

"Why didn't you ever tell me?" he asked. It was something he'd needed to know. Something that filled in some of his empty places hearing it now. "I needed to hear it."

His dad wrung his shaking hands together. "Because I'm not good with stuff like that. I feel it in my chest, but I have trouble making the words come out. That's not an excuse. I understand that but…I guess while you were worried you were disappointing me, I was worried about the same thing when it came to you. I never felt like the dad you deserved. I couldn't give you the things you wanted. Hell, I didn't even talk to you the way I should have. I always felt like I failed you…like I let you down, especially when I had to stop working. When I couldn't pay to get you into the school you deserved or…"

And then his father looked down, and for the first time in Matt's life, he saw him cry. His shoulders shook as he silently let the tears fall, and then it was his dad who stood. His dad who hobbled over and sat next to Matt. His dad who pulled Matt into a hug and held him so damn tightly, Matt struggled to breathe.

"You have nothing to feel bad about. I was so lucky to grow up with you as a role model. You showed me what hard work is. Dedication…and love." His father had worked so hard because he loved his family. Because he wanted to take care of them.

"I love you, son. I'm so damn proud of you."

"I love you too," Matt told him, squeezing his father just as tightly as his dad hugged him.

When they pulled apart, they talked some more. When his mom got home, she joined in. They talked about anything and everything—more of how Matt had felt. About the surgery he'd almost decided against but said he wanted to hear how Matt felt about it first. His dad told Matt some of his favorite stories about Matt growing up, and they laughed.

They were going to be okay. They were going to be more than okay, and for the first time in Matt's life, he saw himself in his dad, and he knew his dad saw himself in Matt too.

OLIVER'S FINGERS MOVED rapidly across the keyboard.

He'd finished his last Davis novel about three weeks before, and then he'd been hit with a new idea so powerfully that he practically had to force himself away from his computer on a daily basis.

This book wasn't about a sexy FBI agent, and it wasn't about a man who loved music.

No, this book was for himself. He was writing his first romance and it felt good...right. Like it fit. He planned to use the pen name he'd created for Matt's book, one he'd now made public.

It wasn't often that Oliver did something that was just for him. He'd been trying to do that—hiking more, writing what he wanted, and he'd even attempted online dating. He hadn't found anyone he liked enough to meet yet, but it was a start.

Austin had also set him up at the LGBT center where he worked so Oliver could volunteer. Oliver enjoyed helping people, being there for them. Yes, he wanted to do things for himself, but the work he did at the center was for him too. It made him feel like he was doing something important, something that mattered. He'd also looked into teaching a writing class. Things hadn't completely unfolded there yet, but he had hopes that they would.

Oliver stared at the screen as words flew across it. He heard the faint ring of his doorbell in the background but did his best to block out the sound. He hated getting interrupted when he was in the zone—when words flew from his fingertips and settled into his chest like nothing he'd written in years, maybe ever.

The doorbell rang for the second time, fighting to interrupt his flow.

He would drive himself crazy if he didn't just get up and answer it. He'd wonder who it was or what he missed, so Oliver hit save and made his way to the front door. When he pulled it open, a piece of paper fluttered to the ground. He caught movement from the corner of his eye, looked up and saw Matt standing in the walkway, his hands in his pockets.

"Hey...I figured you must be writing. I didn't want to interrupt. I can come back."

Oliver didn't answer right away. He took a moment to take Matt in. His cheeks had filled out slightly. His eyes looked brighter. He looked...better. Happier. More like the Matt he'd known growing up. Damn, it felt good to see him like that.

"I can take a short break. Not too long, though." Because this was important to him—working on this book. Taking time for himself. "Come in." He stood back and waited for Matt to head his way. They hadn't spoken at all since Matt left. Oliver had made it a point not to call Matt. If Matt wanted him, he could get ahold of Oliver, himself. And he hadn't, until now. A hundred questions overcrowded his brain. What was he doing back? How long was he here? Why?

When Matt stepped inside, Oliver picked up the note and closed the door behind him. "There's some coffee in the kitchen. Would you like a cup?" Oliver heard the distance in his own question. Like Matt was an old acquaintance rather than one of his closest friends. It felt strange talking to Matt that way.

"Sure. Thanks, Ollie. That'd be nice."

The two of them walked into the kitchen. Matt followed him to the cabinet and when Oliver brought down a coffee mug, he took it. They each poured themselves a cup, doctored it and then sat at the bar.

Oliver waited. This was Matt's show. He'd come to talk and Oliver would listen.

"I got into town yesterday. Had a good talk with my dad—just the two of us. I told him how I feel...how I've always felt. Learned a lot. We're a lot alike, my dad and me."

No shit, Oliver wanted to say, but he didn't. The truth was, a feather could knock him off the barstool right now, he was so surprised. "Wow...that's great, Matty. I'm happy for you. I'm proud of you."

Matt cocked his head slightly toward Oliver and gave him that smile that could always knock Oliver on his ass. Jesus, he did something to Oliver's insides.

"Thanks. I'm proud of me too." He paused, took a drink of his coffee and then said, "You were right, ya know? You feel bad about what you said to me that last night, there's not a doubt in my mind about that, but you were right and I needed to hear it."

There wasn't a part of Oliver that doubted that he had been right, but still…

"I could have said it in a different way. You deserved better than that."

Matt shook his head. "I wouldn't have heard it any other way. Hell, I don't even know if I heard it that night, but eventually I did. That and when you told me good-bye."

"I—" Oliver started but Matt put a hand on his leg.

"Can I go first? I need to do this, Ollie. For me and for you."

Oliver's pulse sped up. He wasn't sure what to think or feel but he nodded, waiting for Matt to continue because the truth was, he needed for Matt to go first too. There was a lot of history that needed to get settled between them.

"I've been going to see a therapist once a week. I've been doing group therapy too. I was depressed…struggling for a long time but I never let myself see it. I tried to pretend it wasn't there. Maybe I've been pretending most of my life."

Oliver swallowed. He sure as shit hadn't expected to hear that. There was truth to his words, though and as he looked at Matt, he noticed small differences in him. The way he sat straighter. The light in his eyes. "Is it helping?" he asked, even though he was sure it was.

"Yeah, Ollie. It's helping." He took another drink of his coffee, Oliver had a feeling, as a way to give himself a moment. "I've learned a lot about myself—losing you and admitting shit I tried to keep buried."

"You didn't lose me. I'll always be your friend."

"I did lose you, though, and that's okay. It needed to happen. Fuck, I have always wanted you. Always. Even before we became friends when I used to see you with Chance and Miles. I wanted nothing more than to be a part of what they had with you. Wanted it so fucking much that I fought against you, against every action you made to try and be my friend, up until that day with the piano."

The muscles in Oliver's stomach spasmed, and his pulse kicked up even more as he listened to Matt.

"Then we became friends, and I wouldn't let myself ever feel like I was enough for you. Jesus, you're the best person I know. You're music to me, like you live right here in my chest." He patted his heart, and Oliver wanted nothing more than to pull him close. To tell him he was enough but he needed to let Matt do this for both of them.

"I think a part of me resented you because I knew you loved me. I've always known, but I didn't understand why. I didn't see *how* you could love me, so I fought against it. I'd falter and pull you close then distance myself again."

Oliver cleared his throat. "And now?"

"Now I'm learning to love myself. I realize that I'm worth it— that my happiness is worth fighting for. I stopped modeling. I've been composing like crazy. I've been working on me, and I'm still a work in progress, but I realized I can fight for everything else, but none of it will ever feel like enough if I don't at least try to fight for you too. Maybe that's selfish of me. Maybe I should let you go, but you never gave up on me, Ollie. For years you've held on, and I'll be damned if I'm going to give up on you this easily. I—"

"Shut up," Oliver interrupted him. "Just shut up." *This* was the Matt he knew. This was the Matt he'd always believed in. This was the Matt he'd always loved. The one he was damned proud of. "It's always been you for me."

"I'm so fucking gone for you, Ollie. It's always been you for me too."

Matt pushed to his feet; he wedged himself between Oliver's thighs. Put his hand against Oliver's cheek and then slid it over to rest on the back of his neck. "I'm sorry it took me so long to get here." He smiled at Oliver, and damned if he couldn't help but return it.

"Better late than never," Oliver replied. "Gone for me…I like it. I'm going to hold you to that, remind you that you said it every chance I get." Jesus, this felt good. Hearing this. Having this.

"You don't have to remind me. I love you. I've loved you for as long as I can remember and if you'll let me, I'll spend every day of my life making up for the time we lost."

But they hadn't really lost it, had they? That was life. Sometimes shortcuts presented themselves but other times, you had to take the long way home. It didn't matter how they got here; what mattered was that they'd arrived. This was their story, and it was better than anything Oliver ever could have written. It was real. It was theirs. And he damn sure couldn't wait to keep on living life with this man by his side.

"There's nothing to make up for. We're exactly where we're supposed to be. I love you too. Now, come here. I really want to taste you."

Matt grinned, leaned in and gave Oliver his mouth. He tasted happiness on Matt's tongue and knew Matt tasted it on his as well.

Oliver had always been the romantic. The one who led with his heart. He'd been battered and bruised but holding Matt, it was all worth it.

EPILOGUE

MATT SAT BESIDE Miles in their booth at Wild Side.

Chance and Oliver were on the dance floor, Chance having dragged Oliver out with him. Now that they were out there, though, Matt could tell his boyfriend was enjoying himself. He loved seeing Oliver have fun.

Matt had been back in Los Angeles for about five weeks now. He'd moved into Oliver's place with him. They'd converted one of the spare rooms into a music room for Matt, which he'd insisted he pay for, himself.

He had a bit of a savings, enough to get him by for a while. He and Oliver spent their days writing—Oliver in his office working on his book and Matt in his music room, composing music.

It was perfect. They were happy. Matt had enrolled in school to get his bachelor's in music, something he should have done a long time ago. He'd also continued with therapy since he'd been here.

"He's happy," Miles said from beside him.

Matt couldn't have been more surprised to hear Miles say that. "Yeah…we both are. I know you don't approve. I know you think I'll hurt him or that I don't deserve him but—"

"You deserve him," Miles interrupted. Matt sure as shit hadn't expected that either. "If you would have asked me a few months ago if I ever thought I'd say that, my answer would have been no. But you're different now…and you love him. A fool can see that. I want him happy too. I want you both happy."

"Thank you," Matt replied. "That means a lot to me." And it did. He'd always wanted Miles's respect. He was a good man. Matt had never doubted that.

"Ollie! Get your ass back here!" Chance said as Oliver sat down in the booth. Looked like that conversation was over.

"I need a drink. You'll be fine out there by yourself." Oliver picked up Matt's glass and finished what was in it. They'd been to Wild Side every Friday night since Matt had been back. The first night had been a little awkward, but things got better each week. He'd gotten to where he looked forward to their Friday night routine.

This was the kind of thing they used to talk about when they were kids—the four of them still being friends and enjoying nights in West Hollywood. It had taken Matt a while to feel like he truly belonged at this table with these men, but there wasn't a doubt in his mind now.

"You have an admirer," Oliver told Miles and then nodded toward the bar.

Miles looked over—they all did—and sure enough, there was a gorgeous man with dark hair eyeing him.

Matt watched him for a moment, and he could have sworn he saw recognition in the other man's face. Then he gave Miles a slight nod. Matt opened his mouth to ask Miles if he knew him, but Miles turned away.

"Oooh, he's pretty. Can I have him?" Chance asked, and Matt let his question go.

"Have at him," Miles told him.

"No. What about you? I seem to remember you giving me shit for years about my sex and love life. Now that I'm happy, I think it's time to focus on you," Oliver told them and everyone laughed except Miles.

"Bite your tongue. Plus, I was never the one who wanted a love life. A sex life works fine for me and how do you know I'm not getting mine?"

"Are you?" Chance asked.

Chance and Miles went back and forth, arguing with each other. Matt leaned back, watching them, enjoying his night.

It was only a moment later that Oliver leaned close. "Why are you being so quiet?" he asked before he pressed a quick kiss to Matt's lips.

"Just thinking," he replied. "Wishing I would have been here a long time ago."

"You're here now," Oliver reminded him.

And he was. And he would spend every day of his life fighting to be as happy as he was right now.

THE END

Continue reading for a sneak peek at book two in the Wild Side series.

PROLOGUE

MILES SORENSON LAY in a bed that wasn't his own. A soft, steady snore came from the man beside him, his arm thrown over his face, his spent cock, flaccid in a nest of dark pubic hair. Hair that Miles had felt scratch his face as he'd taken Quinn's dick deep into his mouth—the scent of sex, musk, and man as he'd blown him.

He should get out of this bed right now. It was late Sunday afternoon, and Miles didn't make a habit of hanging around after he fucked someone. He sure as shit didn't make a habit of spending a whole weekend with someone the way he'd done with Quinn the past couple of days.

Still, he didn't get up, instead trying to figure out why, other than the fact that Quinn was sexy and a good lay, he still lay in this bed, two days after meeting up with him late on a Friday night.

He'd separated from his friends at the corner outside of Wild Side, the bar they met up at every Friday night, but instead of going home like he usually did, he'd made his way to another bar, where he saw a man sitting at a table by himself.

They'd made eye contact and the second they did, Miles saw the interest in the other man's face. He'd walked right over, sat down with him, and now he was in Quinn's bed two days later.

Quinn rolled over and slung his arm over Miles's torso. He only knew the man's first name the same way Quinn only knew he was Miles. They hadn't bothered with surnames. What was the point?

Neither of them planned to see each other past this weekend.

They'd both needed to fuck, done it and there wasn't much more to the story than that. They hadn't only fucked, though—had they? They'd talked too. Not about important shit but they talked more than Miles spoke to most people other than his best friends, Chance, Oliver, and Matt.

"You're thinking hard," Quinn mumbled into Miles's side.

"How do you know that? You met me two days ago, and you can read my moods now?" He spoke with a smile, but it was a serious question. Maybe they'd fucked and talked for two days straight but they didn't really *know* each other. It wasn't like they spoke about anything important.

"I feel it in your muscles. Your body's tight, and your breathing changes. I pay attention to these things." Quinn sat up, his elbow on the bed, looking down at Miles. He had these soft, compassionate, brown eyes. It was one of the first things Miles had noticed about him when they met in the bar—his kind eyes. Such a fucking cliché—meeting a man at a bar and banging his brains out all weekend.

"Yeah? And I'm pretty sure that's the first time you slept for more than half an hour at a time. I pay attention to shit too. Wanna talk about that?" Miles cocked a brow at Quinn and saw him frown.

"No, no I don't."

"Didn't think so. Don't call me on my shit, and I won't call you on yours."

"Yes, sir. Jesus, you're a bossy bastard. That is so fucking hot. I sort of want to go ass up for you again."

Miles chuckled. He sort of wanted to play with Quinn's hungry, little hole again too. The man was something else, that was for sure. But instead of taking Quinn up on his offer he said, "I should go."

"*Finally*," Quinn replied and then winked at him. "I never thought I'd get you out of here. You didn't fall in love with me, did you?"

Miles chuckled. "Fuck no. You didn't fall in love with me, did you?" he teased back; something about Quinn brought it out in him.

"No, baby. There's plenty of dick in West Hollywood."

"Yeah, but I know how to lay the good pipe," Miles replied, almost feeling like he was stalling, which was fucking ridiculous.

"You're a fucking machine. I've never had it so good. Though my head still stings from how hard you pulled my hair." Quinn rubbed a hand over Miles's chest, his white skin a contrast to Miles's darker skin.

"You liked it," Miles countered. He'd always liked things a little rough in bed.

"Did I say I didn't?" Quinn replied.

Instead of keeping their teasing going Miles again said, "I should go."

Quinn nodded and sat up. Miles made his way to the edge of the bed, sitting there with his back to Quinn. His bones felt like they weighed a million pounds. Like he couldn't hold himself up but then he realized he was being incredibly dramatic for no fucking reason and pushed his ass out of the bed and got dressed. There was a rustling sound behind him, and he knew Quinn was doing the same thing.

Five minutes later, they stood at the front door of Quinn's apartment.

"I know the two days wasn't really in the plan but it worked out okay," Quinn told him. He looked tired, like he needed some more sleep.

Miles glanced around the apartment. There were computers and video game shit on an L-shaped table in the corner. Dishes sat on the kitchen counter. They'd taken breaks between fucking to eat, but that was about all they'd done—fucked, rested, eaten, showered, then repeated the process again and again. Quinn's ass had to be killing him, but they'd opted for blowjobs too. He didn't know how either of them had managed to get it up as many times as they had.

"Yeah, it did," Miles finally answered him. "Thanks for the good time."

"Thank you for the same thing," Quinn replied. Miles leaned forward, took his mouth one more time; their tongues tangled before Miles took control. When he'd had his taste, he pulled back, winked at Quinn and then walked away.

That had been just the distraction he'd needed.

Continue reading for a sneak peek at the prequel to the Wild Side series.

CHAPTER ONE

"IT SMELLS LIKE BURNED POPCORN. Did you burn the popcorn again?"

Austin Thompson looked toward his front door just as Dare Nichols closed it. They'd been neighbors and good friends for six years. About two years ago, they'd started having movie or card nights—one or two Sundays a month. It hadn't taken long before one or two Sundays turned into three, and finally they ended up making it their weekly staple.

And a few weeks ago was the one and only time Austin could remember burning the popcorn, but of course Dare had mentioned it every Sunday since. "The popcorn's not burned," Austin grumbled.

"Smells burned."

"No, it doesn't."

"Yes, it does."

"No, it doesn't." Austin glanced at the perfectly popped kernels in his large glass bowl. He didn't mess with that microwave shit. He made it on the stove, the way you were supposed to. His popcorn was perfect, damn it.

"Made ya look!" Dare teased.

Austin rolled his eyes at his friend. The man acted like a ten-year-old trapped in a lunatic's body. "You're giving me a headache."

But he really wasn't. The thing was, he kept Austin on his toes. If he was being honest, he didn't know how they were such good friends because they didn't have much in common. Austin was a youth counselor at an LGBT center. Dare owned a bar. Austin liked to spend his spare time reading; Dare definitely hadn't gotten his name from books. He loved doing anything thrilling. He loved extreme sports and taking risks, and Austin left that up to Dare and the characters in his books.

Despite all of that, Dare was probably one of the best friends he'd ever had—minus the probably.

Dare walked over and ruffled Austin's dark red hair like he was a kid.

"Stop it." Austin jerked his head back, and Dare laughed—deep and sincere, with a husky edge to it. He had the happiest laugh Austin had ever heard—full of life and energy.

"You know you love me."

Austin stared at him and Dare continued, "Grab the popcorn and I'll get the beer. It's your turn to pick the movie. I hope we're watching something good." Dare opened the fridge and pulled out two bottles of beer. "I'm not tired, so hopefully you didn't pick something that'll put me to sleep."

They wouldn't be Austin and Dare if Dare didn't always try to bust his balls. "What's with you? You're being extra obnoxious tonight." Austin nudged Dare's arm. He had his shirt off and wore only a pair of sweats. Like it always did, his thick, brown hair looked styled...but not. It was like he ran his hands through it, made it stick up in just the right way, but it never looked like he put product in it. Knowing Dare he said, "Stay," and his hair just listened. He had that kind of magnetism.

"I'm in a good mood. Can't I be in a good mood?" Dare kicked the fridge closed and turned for the living room. It was a small apartment—both of theirs were, the layouts exactly the same only flipped. That and Austin's had bookshelves and paintings, while Dare had a surfboard in one of the living room corners and his mountain bike by the door and all of the other shit Dare had that he didn't.

Austin followed him into the living room, and they each took a seat on Austin's brown leather couch. Dare looked over and gave him a cocky grin, making Austin say, "Jesus, again? How in the hell do you find all these men to hook up with?" Dare was relentless in his quest for ass—or cock. He didn't discriminate in how he got his sex and most men gladly gave it to him.

"There are these things called hookup apps. You make a profile and browse other people's. You find someone who's hot, talk a bit, or *don't* and there you go. It's really advanced technology. You should try it sometime."

For the second time since Dare came over, Austin rolled his eyes at the man. "You're funny. Has anyone told you you're funny? A regular fucking comedian." He shook his head. "I don't have time to hook up with random people."

"There's always time to fuck."

He knew Dare was half-kidding, but serious as well. The thing was, Austin worked a lot. And even when he wasn't *officially* at work, he was often at the center. He liked spending time with the teens there, liked playing games with them and talking to them, and being a positive role model in their lives. "Plus, I'm seeing Brian, remember?" Well, he was sort of seeing the man. It had been about two months now. They met at one of his favorite West Hollywood coffeehouses. Austin wasn't completely sure how things were going. It wasn't serious, but it was nice to have someone there from time to time. It was nice to feel wanted.

"How's that going, anyway?" Dare reached over, grabbed a handful of popcorn from the bowl on Austin's lap and tossed it into his mouth.

"Good, I think. We have a lot in common. The conversation never stops when we're together. I haven't seen him as much the past couple weeks as I had been, but we're getting ready for the upcoming Rainbow Prom at the center, so I've been spending some extra time there. He understands." Or at least Austin thought he did. He had been a little frustrated when Austin told him he couldn't hang out tonight, but this was his and Dare's tradition. Even Dare skipped out on his wild adventures or sex with random men on Sunday evenings. This was their thing, so he couldn't cancel it. "He's a good man."

"Oh shit, are you going to go and fall in love with this guy?" Dare asked, a strange twinge to his voice that Austin hadn't heard before.

"What? No." Austin shook his head. "I like him, though. As I said, we have a lot in common. He doesn't think my choice in movies would put him to sleep," Austin teased. Really, if there was a form with questions for the kind of man who would be perfect for Austin, he was pretty sure Brian would check every box that should be marked.

"Hmm." Dare reached over for more popcorn. "I'm not sure I like him. He definitely doesn't like me. He looked at me like I was something he stepped in, the bastard. He seems a little boring in my book, and like an asshole. Assholes are usually fun. If you make ass boring, there's something wrong with you."

"Oh, great, Dare. I just said he and I have a lot in common, and now you say he's an ass. Spending time with you really boosts my self-esteem." Austin set the bowl of popcorn on the table and crossed his arms. He was being ridiculous, and he wasn't sure why. The truth was, hearing Dare say that made his insides twist up. He'd always felt boring and sure didn't want to hear that someone he related to had a quality he'd always feared was his.

"Shut up." Dare nudged him. "You know I don't think you're boring or an ass—the bad kind of ass, at least. We balance each other out, and when you *do* pick a movie I don't love or want to

213

stay home to read a book, you get the best-friend pass."

Austin opened his mouth to tell Dare to fuck off, but Dare spoke again. "I never really had a best friend before you."

He closed his mouth. Opened it. Closed it again. Dare didn't offer much of himself, and nothing of his past. Hell, Austin didn't even know his real first name. It used to be that Austin asked him all the time what his name was, but Dare would never tell him. He was still curious but he'd come to accept it. For Dare to have said that about Austin was a big deal. "I…"

"Shut up. Let's not get sappy here. Put the movie on before I veto you and choose one of my own." Dare leaned forward, grabbed the bowl of popcorn and started to eat from it again. Austin knew the conversation had ended, and the moment was gone. Still, he couldn't stop thinking about it all night. How did he get so lucky to be Dare's first real friend? And how could that be true when everyone in the world loved Dare, gravitated toward him and his electric personality? It didn't make sense, but then, that was Dare.

THE BAR WAS WILD TONIGHT.

He loved it when Wild Side was like this. Yeah, they were busy every night—men and women came in to dance, drink, stick money in the underwear of go-go boys *and* girls, because Dare believed in having something here for the ladies too—but the place was alive with energy tonight.

It had been the perfect Friday. He'd spent the morning on the ocean and the evening in his bar. He never would have thought he'd have this kind of life—the kind where good shit happened more often than bad shit. He'd worked hard to be the man he was, hard to make it so he wasn't like the family he'd been raised with.

And he'd done it. Every time he looked around Wild Side, he couldn't believe he'd really fucking done it.

He had no clue what made him think about his past tonight. It was probably the comment he'd let slip with Austin the other night. He wasn't even sure why he'd said it. He was usually pretty good at keeping things like that closed tight. What was the purpose of dwelling on the past? Or feeling sorry for yourself? Dare liked to have fun, to skirt the rules and take risks. He was much more interested in enjoying his life now than focusing on anything else.

Fucking Austin made shit like that sneak out every once in a while.

Speaking of the man, Dare weaved his way through the mass of bodies dancing to Britney, pulling out his phone as he did. Austin picked up before Dare made it out of the main part of the bar.

"Hello?" he answered.

"Hey!"

"I can't hear you, Dare. I need to go anyway. Brian's on his way!" he yelled through the line.

"Wait!" Dare rushed out, not sure why he needed to talk to Austin right now. He made his way toward the locked door, nodded at the security guard and then unlocked it and slipped inside. Once he was in the hallway that led to his soundproofed office, he spoke again. "What are you guys doing tonight? You should take a walk on the wild side and come to the bar." Not that he thought Brian would. He wasn't sure Wild Side was Brian's kind of place. It wasn't technically Austin's either but he'd come from time to time.

"Did you really just say we should take a walk on the wild side? That's corny, even for you."

"I thought it was cute," Dare countered, and Austin chuckled. "The place is on fire tonight. Come down, check it out. Tell Brian drinks are on the house." They were probably doing something like having a late dinner and a quiet glass of wine somewhere, because Dare had no doubt that Austin had probably worked late tonight.

He was fiercely loyal to the LGBT center and the people there. Dare respected the hell out of him for it. He gave Austin shit but it was probably one of his favorite things about his friend.

"I'll see if he's interested, but I doubt it," Austin told him, and Dare rolled his eyes. That was a no.

"You suck."

"I swallow too," Austin countered, to Dare's surprise. He chuckled. Austin was in a good mood tonight. Dare could hear it in the playfulness of his voice. He must really like this Brian guy, which Dare had to admit, he didn't get. Not just because he didn't think Brian was good enough for Austin, but Dare didn't understand the need for monogamy and love and all that shit. He just wasn't wired that way.

Austin was, though, and while Dare should be happy that his friend was in a relationship that could eventually be serious, he wasn't. It just didn't feel right. Sure, on paper Brian seemed like the kind of man that Austin would want, but his gut twisted when he thought about Austin with him. He didn't trust Brian. He hadn't been lying when he said he didn't think Brian liked him, and he'd be damned if he'd lose his friendship with Austin over something stupid like an asshole in a suit.

Which was what he was being right now. Stupid. And kind of an asshole. Why in the hell was he thinking about all this shit? "Fine, go out, drink wine and eat steak and suck dick while I'm working. I see how you are." Though he wasn't averse to taking someone back to his office if he found a man who wanted to suck dick too.

"Thanks for the permission, and I'm sure you've sucked cock while I was working more often than the other way around."

"Yeah, but—"

"Brian's here," Austin cut him off. "Have a good one," he told Dare before the phone went dead. Dare stared at it in disbelief.

Austin had never hung up on him before.

Okay, he was being really fucking strange, and he didn't know why. Dare shoved the phone back into his pocket and turned around to go back the way he'd come.

He had a busy bar out there, full of all sorts of fun and trouble. Even though he owned Wild Side and didn't have to be on the floor, he loved being out there in the middle of things, serving drinks and talking to people right along with his staff.

He'd go out there and find his own fun like he always did.

Acknowledgement

As always, I have to thank my readers. I couldn't do this without you. I am thankful for you every day. Thanks to my family. You put up with a lot from me.

My beta readers, thanks for the input and my editors and proofers for helping me make it pretty. Also, thank you to Sarah Jo Chreene for the gorgeous artwork.

About the Author

Riley Hart is the girl who wears her heart on her sleeve. She's a hopeless romantic. A lover of sexy stories, passionate men, and writing about all the trouble they can get into together. If she's not writing, you'll probably find her reading.

Riley lives in California with her awesome family, who she is thankful for every day.

Other books by Riley Hart

Weight of the World
Faking It

Crossroads Series:
Crossroads
Shifting Gears
Test Drive
Jumpstart

Rock Solid Construction series:
Rock Solid

Broken Pieces series:
Broken Pieces
Full Circle
Losing Control

Blackcreek series:
Collide
Stay
Pretend

Manufactured by Amazon.ca
Bolton, ON